"Sigmund Brouwer's masterful storytelling and eye for detail turn *Fortress of Mist* into a grand—and harrowing—adventure for every reader. You'll feel the grime of castle dungeons, the sting of sword blades, and the elation of victory. It's a story full of surprising twists, shocking betrayals, and baffling mysteries. But at its heart, this book is about courage, wisdom, and hope—and losing yourself in a fabulous story well told."

—ROBERT LIPARULO, author of *The 13th Tribe, The Judgment Stone,* and the Dreamhouse Kings series

"Sigmund Brouwer spins an exciting story with *Fortress of Mist,* full of classic elements and clever twists. His style is reminiscent of the wonderful Lloyd Alexander, and I felt both comfortably familiar with the unfolding story and pleasantly surprised by new plot developments. As the young orphan hero struggling to establish himself as ruler in a world of courtly intrigues and dangerous Druids, Thomas will appeal to boys and girls, young and old. Brouwer keeps us guessing, and I was particularly interested by his use of scientific "magic." An engaging read that will leave readers eager to pick up the next volume."

—ANNE ELISABETH STENGL, author of the award-winning Tales of Goldstone Wood series

"From the first line, readers will be hooked into this page-turning adventure. An engaging and compelling read."

—DEBBIE VIGUIÉ, author of *Kiss of Death*

Fortress of Mist

◆ BOOK TWO ◆
MERLIN'S IMMORTALS

Sigmund Brouwer

WATERBROOK
PRESS

Fortress of Mist
Published by WaterBrook Press
12265 Oracle Boulevard, Suite 200
Colorado Springs, Colorado 80921

ISBN 978-1-4000-7155-5
ISBN 978-0-307-73122-7 (electronic)

Published in the United States by WaterBrook Multnomah, an imprint of the Crown Publishing Group, a division of Random House Inc., New York.

WaterBrook and its deer colophon are registered trademarks of Random House Inc.

Library of Congress Cataloging-in-Publication Data
Brouwer, Sigmund, 1959–
     Fortress of mist : a novel / Sigmund Brouwer.—First edition.
          pages cm.—(Merlin's immortals ; book 2)
     Merlin's immortals is a revised and expanded version of The winds of light series.
     ISBN 978-1-4000-7155-5 (alk. paper)—ISBN 978-0-307-73122-7 (electronic)
     [1. Druids and druidism—Fiction. 2. Knights and knighthood—Fiction. 3. Civilization, Medieval—Fiction. 4. Christian life—Fiction. 5. Great Britain—History—Medieval period, 1066-1485—Fiction.] I. Title.
     PZ7.B79984Fp 2013
     [Fic]—dc23
                                                2012039449

Printed in the United States of America
2013—First Edition

10 9 8 7 6 5 4 3 2 1

MIDSUMMER, NORTHERN ENGLAND—AD 1312

Thomas woke to a kiss on the forehead from a woman he once believed he had loved, a woman who had betrayed and spied upon him, a woman he had watched die.

But now, in the light of the single candle she held, she looked down upon him and smiled.

Isabelle.

"Thomas," she whispered. "Thomas, I have returned."

He tried to rub his face, but it felt as though his arms were pressed against his side. And because movement seemed nearly impossible, he told himself that he was still in the dream he'd been having before she kissed him.

In the dream, he'd been standing upon the same crest where he had seen the kingdom of Magnus for the first time.

At that initial sighting, the island in the center of the lake that protected Magnus had been placid, reflecting the sheep- and cattle-dotted hills that surrounded it. Then, the high stone walls that ringed the island and protected those inside had cast shadow onto the narrow drawbridge that made a full attack impossible.

In his dream, this was not how Magnus had appeared. In his dream, it had looked as it did on some of the mornings when Thomas would climb to a high point and wait for the sun to break over the opposite side of the valley, watching shrouds of gray swirl upward from the water to hide the walls, so that the castle appeared to be a fortress of mist.

In his dream, he felt the same undefinable loneliness of yearning that drove him to sit in solitude and wait for the sun to burn away the mist and reveal the unmistakable reality of stone and iron that Thomas had conquered. In his dream, he still knew the truth: Sarah, his mother and the one who taught him of his destiny, had died. William, the knight who'd become a friend and mentor, was gone. Katherine, the first person in Magnus he could trust, had disappeared. In his dream, he felt as he did in waking—that the victorious joy he felt as the rightful heir of his reclaimed kingdom had dissolved into the burdens of duty, no differently than the mists evaporated in sunlight.

In his dream, he'd heard a voice from the mist calling his name, until the softness of lips against his forehead had pulled him from the mists and brought him the realization that it was Isabelle.

"Thomas," she whispered. "Thomas, I have returned."

More awake now, Thomas told himself to reach under his pillow for the dagger he kept there as protection. While soldiers guarded the only door into his bedchamber, high up in the castle, Magnus still contained too much mystery. Trust, he had early decided, was a dangerous luxury, and he always slept with a weapon nearby.

With great effort, he pulled his arms away from his body, yet it felt as if his hands were moving through warm tar. He let out a deep breath and tried to sit, but could move no further. His silk sleeping gown rustled softly as he tried to move, but it felt like a giant hand held him in place, squeezing him at the waist. What was happening to him? Could it be that he still dreamed, but dreamed that he was awake?

"Thomas," Isabelle said, her voice too clear, too urgent, to be the work of his sleeping mind. "I offer no harm. We must speak."

Shadows of the candle flickered across her face.

Impossible. He had seen the blow that had crushed her skull.

Her death had occurred shortly after Thomas had brought Isabelle for an audience, to interrogate her for her actions in the days just before and just after he had won the kingdom. He had been leaning forward to absorb the words he would never forget.

"Thomas, there is a great circle of conspiracy. Much larger than you and I…and there is much at stake.… Haven't you wondered why this castle is set so securely, so far away from the outer world? Why would anyone bother attacking a village here? Yet an impenetrable castle was founded. And by no less a wizard than Merlin."

That's when the door had exploded open. A man, rushing toward them with a short club extended, the guards on his heels. The man swinging the club before Thomas could dive forward. Isabelle, motionless with blood matting her hair. Her attacker had worn the peculiar cross symbol on his ring that matched the medallion hanging on a chain around Isabelle's neck.

Hours later, her head bandaged but still unconscious, Isabelle's ragged breathing had slowed, then stopped, and she had died in his arms while the doctor looked on, shaking his head grimly, his fingers still stained with her blood.

"Thomas, there is a great circle of conspiracy…much at stake."

The woman who had blurted those words before dying now stood before him, holding a candle, speaking his name.

Impossible.

His tongue felt fat and sandy in his mouth. "Who are you?"

"You know."

"Tell me anyway."

"You know who I am. I am your Isabelle."

His head was clearing, and as it did, an idea came. He had known very little about the young woman who had beguiled him on the journey to conquering Magnus. While it didn't explain how the woman in front of him had made it past the soldiers outside his bedchamber, perhaps there was an explanation for why it appeared Isabelle was now alive.

"Tell me too," Thomas said, "about the time I fell into a stream and you helped me out of the water. How did I thank you for it?"

"On our journey to Magnus from the gallows?"

Thomas nodded and tried to lean forward. She was about to fail his test. He was certain. There could be no explanation other than she was a fraud. Surely this was Isabelle's secret twin sister, trying to deceive him.

She smiled. "Your memory fails you," she said. "It was not you, but I who fell into the stream."

No, his memory had not failed him. He could still picture her clearly, how she looked after he had pulled her from the water, how their eyes had met with much unspoken between them.

"So you did not thank me," she said, her voice hypnotic and low. "I thanked you. I kissed the tips of my fingers, like this." She lifted her hand to her mouth. "And then I touched them to your mouth, like this." She softly brushed her fingers across his lips, sending a jolt of warmth and awareness through the foggy weight that held him. "I remember clearly, because it was the first time I realized that I could pledge my heart to you."

Only Isabelle could have known about that quiet moment at the stream, and it was beyond likelihood that she would have reason to share it, even with her twin.

Which meant there was no twin.

Which meant the woman in front of him truly must be Isabelle.

Two

Y ou are dead," Thomas told the woman with the candle.

He felt the first shiver of fear. This seemed too real to be a dream, yet he hardly dared trust his senses.

Only an apparition could have entered this heavily guarded room with its solid stone walls in the upper reaches of the castle. Only an apparition could explain that which he saw in front of him.

But could a ghost hold a solid object like a candle? Or could the candle, too, be part of the figment?

"Come closer," Thomas said. "Let me hold your hand."

If this specter meant him harm, it would have done so while he slept. If she was of flesh and bone, he would learn the truth as soon as he could grab hold. Then he would call for his soldiers.

"I will keep my distance," Isabelle said. "My heart is yours, but trust for you is another matter. I believe you were about to have me arrested when I made my confession to you. Before..."

"Before what?"

"You know as well as I do. Before Geoffrey rushed in and clubbed me."

"I will say it then. You died in my arms."

"Yes," she said.

"Then you cannot be you." The words sounded foolish in his own ears, yet what else could he say? The dead did not rise to live again.

"You see me standing in front of you and know who I am. Isabelle. Daughter of Lord Richard Mewburn, the lord of this castle until you conquered it."

"Reclaimed it," Thomas said. "He destroyed my family to take it from them and left me an orphan."

"I cannot change the past. The future depends on the choices you will make as the new lord."

Her earlier words echoed in his mind. *"Haven't you wondered why this castle is set so securely, so far away from the outer world? Why would anyone bother attacking a village here? Yet an impenetrable castle was founded. And by no less a wizard than Merlin."*

"You had been ready to tell me more of Magnus. How it was founded, why it is so secure and isolated, and why the king of England puts no direct authority upon it. You have these answers?"

"Yes," she said. "But I will not give them to you. Not yet."

He wanted to leap from his bed and hold her and shake the answers loose. But his body would not obey him. It felt as though he were bound by an invisible rope.

"Then when?" he asked.

"Soon, you will be given a chance to show allegiance to the symbol."

"Symbol?"

"Don't pretend ignorance, Thomas. It doesn't suit you." She reached inside her cloak and lifted the medallion with the peculiar cross. "You see that I am here. You must believe how much power we have. Join us." She knelt beside his bed, her face close to his. "You and I. Together. We can have it all. We can be the next generation."

Much of what Isabelle said reflected what his own mother had told him all through his childhood. Yet he quickly pushed the thought away. He would not accept that Isabelle and his mother were part of the same mysterious alliance.

"If you know the answers, begin there," Thomas said. "Then I'll decide."

"I am here, in front of you, alive. Isn't that enough? Doesn't that show you the power we have?"

"How would I show allegiance? What will be asked of me?"

"You have something we want."

"Tell me what it is you think I have," he said.

"Don't play childish games. Deliver it, and this kingdom will never be taken from you. Withhold it, and it shall surely be taken away."

His secret library. Books of knowledge, unknown to most of the world. Used correctly, this knowledge was like wizardry. But how could she know that he possessed them?

She rose. "Join us. Join me."

"Not without answers."

"You cannot be given the answers until your allegiance is certain. It was no different for me. Once I showed my loyalty, I was given all."

"Guards!" Thomas croaked. He found his voice and shouted louder. "Guards!"

Both heard the lifting of the outside latch of the door.

Isabelle frowned, and Thomas could not tell if it conveyed anger or sadness. "You disappoint me." Isabelle flung her arm, and the bed-chamber seemed to explode into sunlight. He closed his eyes against the unexpected brightness. When he opened them again, it was dark.

The guards finally opened the door, carrying torches that again filled the bedchamber with light. Traces of smoke drifted through the air, but Isabelle was gone.

❧

In one of the castle's prison cells, far below Thomas's bedchamber, Geoffrey, the village candle maker, gorged himself on cold chicken.

Isabelle had to suppress her urge to vomit. How could he eat in such a disgusting setting? But the small man had always been given to filth—in appearance and habit and thoughts. The squalor of life in the prison cell had only worsened his usual foulness to a point where she could barely breathe. He belched and reached for a goblet of mead to wash down the chicken, then wiped his mouth with his sleeve.

"His answer?" he asked Isabelle. The flame of a small candle enclosed them in a globe of soft light, and she hated the intimacy here as much as she'd enjoyed it earlier with Thomas.

"He called for his guards."

Geoffrey gave her a smug grin. "He refused you. Again. It must be humiliating to learn that your charms won't turn every head."

Isabelle wished—and not for the first time—that she had been the one to club Geoffrey across his bald head, instead of receiving the blow from him.

As much as it galled her, Geoffrey was a shrewd man and a discerning judge of human nature. He seemed to especially enjoy her humiliation. She had not expected to find herself yearning for Thomas, and it had taken her awhile to recognize the sensation of want. Nothing before had been withheld from her in her privileged life as daughter of the previous lord of Magnus.

Indeed, a half hour earlier, in the chamber near the top of the castle while she had been waiting for an answer from Thomas, she had found herself nearly trembling and giddy with anticipation. After a lifetime of being indulged in every whim, when she had wanted one thing more than anything else, it had been denied to her. She could appreciate the irony.

"Shall we simply arrange to have Thomas murdered?" Geoffrey asked. "Would that be a balm to your wounded pride?"

"It is not your decision or mine."

"Interesting," Geoffrey said. She felt as if he were a cat and she an injured mouse in his paws. "I thought that once you were spurned, you would want to see him dead."

"We have been taught, have we not, to set our emotions aside for the greater good of our cause?"

The answer was deflective, of course, and she saw by the widening of his smug grin that Geoffrey understood.

"After all," she continued, "when I told my father I would hang myself if he gave you my hand in secret marriage, you set aside your own humiliation and continued to serve him."

Geoffrey's grin became savage, and for a moment, she wondered if he would leap forward. Truth be told, she hoped for it. She never met with him unless she had a dagger ready and hidden in her sleeve, tipped with poison. If she killed Geoffrey here and now to protect herself, the others of the symbol would understand.

With a visible effort, Geoffrey calmed himself. "Yes," he said. "We both must serve." Then came his turn to lash out. "A shame I needed to nearly kill you for you to learn to reveal nothing about us to the world."

Yes, Isabelle had been on the verge of telling Thomas too much. She didn't know then what she knew now. Of the listening posts hidden in the walls. Of the vastness of the power belonging to those she now served. Of the boundless rewards that came with that power.

"Such a man of sacrifice too," she countered. "Providing the lesson and paying the price for it in prison."

They both knew that Geoffrey could escape at any time. All he had to do was leave the same way that Isabelle would leave with the chicken bones and goblet she had delivered. Those of the symbol knew all the secret passages in the castle. But their enemies knew the passages too.

"When the kingdom is returned to us," he snarled, "you will regret your impertinence. And now that you understand who we are—who I am—I doubt you will choose a rope over my bed next time."

Isabelle fought an outward show of revulsion. "Thomas will choose us. He will choose me." And in so choosing, she would have Thomas for a husband, not this repulsive beast in front of her.

Geoffrey snorted. "This is a man still searching his kingdom for that hideous, worthless freak."

They both knew that Geoffrey meant a girl who had been his servant, whose face had been destroyed by a fire. Katherine. The one, they suspected, who had helped Thomas in his most crucial moment of danger to conquer Magnus.

Isabelle shrugged. "She is of no consequence." Yet her emotions roiled within her. Thomas could have Isabelle at any time, yet the one he sought was a mere beggar with a face too gruesome to be seen. It was because of loyalty, of course, not desire. But still, she hated that another woman should claim any part of Thomas's attention.

"This is a man who lets a sense of justice rule him," Geoffrey said. "Men such as this are dangerous. And we have learned the only way to stop them is to destroy them."

THREE

T*hrust! Thrust! Slash sideways to parry the counterthrust! Thrust again!*

A small group of hardened soldiers watched impassively as Thomas weakened slowly in defense against their captain.

Ignore the dull ache of fatigue that tempts you to lower your sword hand, Thomas commanded himself. *Advance! Retreat! Quickly thrust! Now parry!*

Above Thomas, gray clouds of a cold June day. Around him, a large area of worn grass, and beyond the dirt and grass, the castle keep and village buildings within the walls of Magnus.

Right foot forward with right hand. Concentrate. Blink the sweat from your eyes. And watch his sword hand!

He can sense you weakening. He pushes harder. You cannot fight much longer. Formulate a plan!

To his right, Thomas's eye caught a sprightly boy, no older than twelve, struggling to push through the wall of soldiers blocking him from Thomas. "Thomas!" the boy cried. One burly soldier clamped a massive hand around the boy's arm and held him back.

Thomas began to gasp for air in great ragged gulps. His sword drooped. His quick steps blurred in precision.

The captain, a full hand taller than Thomas, grinned.

The death thrust comes soon! Lower your guard now!

Thomas flailed tiredly, hoping to appear as though he had relaxed a moment too long.

His opponent's grin stretched wider, and brought his sword high to end the fight.

Now!

Thomas focused all his remaining energy on swinging his sword beneath that briefly unguarded upstroke. The impact of sword on ribs jarred his arm to the elbow. He danced back, expecting victory.

Instead, the captain roared with rage as he fell backward onto the dirt and scrabbled to his feet.

"That will cost you dearly!"

Among the soldiers, a few faces showed amusement. The boy among them kicked his captor in the shins but could not free himself.

The captain rushed forward and waved his sword.

Intent on saving what energy he could, Thomas merely held his own sword carefully in front to guard.

"Fool!" the captain shouted, still waving the sword in his right hand as distraction while his left hand flew upward. At the top of that arc, the captain released a fistful of loose dirt into the eyes and mouth of his younger opponent.

Thomas caught most of the dirt as he sucked in a lungful of air. The rest blinded him with pain. A choking retch brought him to his knees, and he felt but did not see the captain's sword flash downward. Once across the side of the ribs. Then a symbolic point thrust in the center of his chest.

Over.

The soldiers hooted and clapped before dispersing to their daily duties. Dirt wiped from his eyes, Thomas recognized his thieving traveling companion, Tiny John, who broke loose as his captor joined the applause.

"That dirt was an unfair thing for him to do, it was!" Tiny John whispered. "You want me to snatch his purse to teach him a lesson?"

In reply, Thomas coughed twice more, then staggered to his feet.

"Wooden swords and horsehide vests aside, my lord," the captain said with a smirk as he approached Thomas, "I expect you'll be taking a few bruises to your bed tonight."

Thomas spit dirt from his mouth. "I expect you'll have one yourself, Robert. It was no light blow I dealt to your ribs. By our rules, the fight should have been ended." He wiped his face and left a great smudge of sweat-oiled dirt.

"Rightfully so. By our rules, you were the winner," Robert of Uleran replied. He was a man nearly into his fourth decade of living, solid and tough. His scarred and broken face was a testimony to the way of battle that he had spent much of his life. When it was set in anger, children would run from that face, screaming. But when he smiled, as he did now, no child could ever be frightened. "I continued, however, for two reasons."

Thomas spit more dirt from his mouth and waited. He felt Tiny John tugging at his sleeve and fidgeting as though he stood on hot coals. He clamped a hand onto the young man's shoulder, hoping to quell Tiny John's wild energy and maintain his own much-needed air of authority.

"One, I was angry you had fooled me. A teacher should never misjudge his student so badly. It's been a month, and you've learned far quicker than most. I should have expected that trick of pretending to weaken from you."

"Anger has never been part of the rules," Thomas observed. Tiny John whined his name, but Thomas held him and paid him no mind.

"Neither has mercy. And do not deny it." Robert's eyes flashed beneath thick, dark eyebrows. "When you landed that first blow, you should have moved in to finish me. Instead, you paused. That hesitation may someday cost you your life."

Robert drew his cloak aside and began to unbind the thick, horse-leather padding around his upper body. "I will not impart to you all I know about fighting, only to have you lose to a lesser man with more cruelty. The dirt in your face, I hope, has proved to be a great lesson."

"Thomas!" Tiny John blurted. Thomas good-naturedly placed a hand over Tiny John's mouth. He intended to use this moment to make his announcement.

"Robert," he said, "it no longer pleases me that you are captain of all these soldiers. Pick your replacement."

The older man's jaw tightened. "My lord, have I offended you?"

"Pick your replacement," Thomas demanded. As lord of Magnus, he could not allow anyone to question his direct orders.

"Yes, my lord," Robert growled through gritted teeth. He inhaled sharply and cleared his throat. "I choose David of Fenway, my lord," Robert said. "He shows great ability and the men respect him."

Robert of Uleran then turned, even though he had not completed the removal of his fighting gear. His obvious anger goaded him to leave quickly.

"Please remove your possessions from the soldiers' quarters," Thomas said.

Robert's face reddened with rage at further insult. His narrow scar lines flushed with blood, and he wheeled quickly and stared at Thomas.

Neither flinched.

Finally Robert's voice rumbled, "Yes, my lord."

Thomas drew his own breath to speak but was interrupted by the drumming of horse's hooves.

A great white beast rounded the buildings opposite the exercise area. On it, a man in a flowing purple cape. Sword sheathed in scabbard. No travel bags attached to the saddle.

Thomas removed his hand from Tiny John's face and placed it on Robert's shoulder to hold his presence.

"The Earl of York," Tiny John blurted. "That's what I was trying to tell you. The most powerful man in the land! He asked permission at the gates to enter alone and unguarded. Twenty of his men remain outside."

Thomas and Robert exchanged glances.

"Wait," Thomas told Robert. "First we go to the ramparts."

Robert nodded, his lips tight. Thomas felt a surge of gratitude at the man's loyalty. Then he turned his attention to the unexpected arrival of the man in the flowing purple cape preparing to dismount from the great white horse.

The Earl of York.

Though tucked in the remotest valley of the North York moors, Magnus still lay within jurisdiction of the Earl of York. Thomas had always known it was only a matter of time until he faced his next challenge as new lord of Magnus. Would the earl accept a new pact of loyalty? Or could he be here to declare war?

Four

The man moved forward. To Robert, he extended his right hand to show it bare of weapons. "Thomas of Magnus, I presume. I am the Earl of York."

Robert's hand remained at his side, clearly in no mood to enjoy the mistake. "The lord of Magnus stands beside me."

The earl's eyes widened briefly with surprise. He recovered quickly and extended his right hand to Thomas.

"I come in peace," he said. "I beg of you to receive me in equal manner."

"We shall extend to you the greatest possible hospitality," Thomas answered. "And I wish for you to greet Robert of Uleran, the man I trust most within Magnus and"—Thomas paused to enjoy the announcement he had been about to make—"the newly appointed sheriff of this manor. He may be busy, however, for the rest of the afternoon, as he is moving his possessions to his new residence in the keep."

If the Earl of York did not understand the reason for Robert's sudden and broad smile, he was polite enough not to ask.

⚜

Thomas, still accompanied by Robert, led the Earl of York and his horse to the stables. There, he summoned a boy to tend to the earl's mount.

It took great willpower not to bombard the Earl with questions. Thomas, however, remembered advice that he had been given by the woman who had raised him: the one who speaks first shows anxiousness and, in so doing, loses ground.

Thomas contented himself with a very ordinary observation. "The clouds promise rain," he said as they left the shelter of the stables.

The Earl of York looked up from his study of the nearby archery range. "I fear much more than rain."

Thomas waited, but the earl said nothing more until their walk brought them to the keep of Magnus.

"A moat within the castle walls?" the earl asked.

In front of them lay a shallow ditch. Had it only been two months since he had filled it with tar and crackling dry wood and threatened to siege the former lord and his soldiers unless they gave up without bloodshed?

"Temporary," Thomas commented, and volunteered no further information. He was in the process of ordering even more protective features to the already famous defenses of the castle. It did not seem prudent to give away secrets.

The earl paused and looked upward at the keep. Four stories high with walls constructed of stone more than three feet thick, it was easily the most imposing structure within the walls of Magnus.

Thomas, too, gazed in appreciation. From its top turrets, he often surveyed the lake that surrounded the castle walls and beyond to the high, steep hills of the moors, etched against the sky. Morning was best, before the wind began and when the endless, low carpet of heather glowed purple in the sun's first rays. He would watch as Magnus began to stir. Shops, each with a large painted sign that showed a symbol that represented its trade, lined the main street. Then the narrow curved streets with houses so cramped together and leaning in all directions like crooked, dirty teeth.

And of course, the small cathedral. Even at a time when he should be alert to the utmost because of the presence of the Earl of York, Thomas couldn't help but turn his eyes and thoughts upon the steeple that rose from the depths of the village. Though as an orphan, Thomas had seen enough of the corruption and wealth of religion to learn to hate it, he smiled because of an old man within its walls. An old man Thomas had once confused for the priest, but who instead had been tasked with sweeping the stone floors there. An old man who truly believed in the God whom Thomas struggled to find, and who seemed to live in a manner that aligned with his belief. Unlike the monks who had raised Thomas as a slave rather than the innocent orphan he was.

Thomas forced his thoughts back to the present moment. He was, after all, standing beside the Earl of York, the most powerful man for hundreds of miles in any direction.

He glanced at the earl to see if he, too, had finished his inspection of the keep. The earl nodded.

Thomas almost smiled at the patronizing demonstration of power. *This man appears to be giving me permission to allow him entry to my hall!*

They climbed the outside steps with Robert following. Tiny John, always easily distracted, had scampered away from them into the village.

The entrance to the keep was twenty feet from the ground, designed to make it difficult for attackers to gain entrance.

The ground level, which could be reached by descending an inside staircase, contained the food stores and the kitchen on one side, the open hall for eating and entertainment on the other. The top three stories of the keep's square design contained residences, with the lord's rooms on the top. All rooms were tucked against the four outer walls, so each level was open in the center and looked down upon the hall. Beneath was the dungeon, so deep below the stone that the cries of prisoners would never reach the hall.

Thomas always shuddered when he pictured that hole of endless night. He had spent much too long there once, almost doomed before he could even start the events that had led to him conquering Magnus. And now—the thought was always on his mind, even as he swung open the great doors of the keep to allow the Earl of York inside—the dungeon held a silent and stubborn prisoner, proving to be one of his thorniest problems as a newly conquering lord.

Until the arrival of the earl.

"May I leave, my lord?" Robert asked.

"As you wish," Thomas said. He would have appreciated the man beside him during a discussion with the earl. But the need for help might show weakness. Thomas was glad that Robert knew it too. It said much for the man's cunning.

Thomas gestured at two leather-padded chairs near the hearth. Before they had time to sit, a maid appeared with two cups containing a steaming mixture of milk, sugar, and crushed barley.

The earl raised an eyebrow. "No wine?"

Disdain?

Thomas remembered the instructions from long ago: never show fear, nor hesitation.

"No wine," Thomas confirmed. "It tends to encourage sloth."

The earl grinned. "There's gentle criticism if I ever heard it. And from one so young."

They studied each other.

Thomas repeated to himself: *Never show fear, nor hesitation.* He wanted to close his eyes briefly to silently thank Sarah, who had spent many hours coaching him on how to behave as a lord. She alone had believed he would someday rule Magnus. And now he faced his first great test. *What does the earl want? What is he thinking?*

His eyes did not leave the earl's face. Thomas saw a man already forty years old, but with a face quite different than one would expect of royalty at that age. The chin had not doubled, or tripled, with good living. No broken veins on his nose to suggest too much enjoyment of wine. No sagging circles beneath his eyes betrayed sleepless nights from poor health or a bad conscience.

Instead, the face was broad and remarkably smooth. Neatly trimmed red-blond hair that spoke of Viking ancestry. Blue eyes that matched the sky just before dusk. Straight, strong teeth that now gleamed in a smile.

Thomas lifted his thick clay cup in a wordless salute. The earl responded in turn and gulped the thick, sweet drink.

Sunlight glinted from the earl's huge gold ring. Thomas froze.

Its symbol was identical to that on Geoffrey's ring and Isabelle's pendant.

FIVE

D o you treat all visitors this harshly?" the earl asked.

"Sir! I beg of you forgiveness. Do you wish to dine immediately?"

"It is hardly the food, or lack thereof. Surely you have questions, yet you force me to begin!"

"Again, I beg of you forgiveness."

"If you want me to believe that, you have to better hide your smile." The earl laughed at the obvious discomfort his statement caused Thomas. "Enough," he then said. "I see you and I shall get along famously. I detest men who offer me their throats like craven dogs."

"Thank you, my lord," Thomas said quietly. He coughed. "I presume you are here to inspect me."

The earl nodded.

"I thought as much," Thomas said. "Otherwise you would not have made such a show of mistakenly greeting my sheriff, Robert."

This time, the earl had enough grace to show discomfort. "My acting was so poor?"

Thomas shook his head. "Between Robert and me, you should have easily guessed which one was young enough to be the new lord of Magnus. Only a fool would have entered Magnus without knowing anything about his future ally—or opponent."

Thomas held his breath.

The Earl of York decided to let the reference to ally or opponent slip past them both. He sipped again from his cup.

"Do your men practice their archery often?"

"With all due respect, my lord," Thomas answered, "I think you mean to question me about the distance between the men and their targets."

This time, the earl did not bother to hide surprise.

"You are a man of observation," Thomas said simply. "And a fighting man. I saw your eyes measure the ground from where the grass was trampled to where the targets stand. I would guess a man with experience in fighting would think it senseless to have practice at such great distance."

"Yes," the earl said. "I had wondered. But I had also reserved judgment."

"I am having the men experiment with new bows."

"New bows?"

Thomas showed the question had been indiscreet by ignoring it. "In so doing, I also wish them to understand that I desire them to survive battles, not die gloriously. Distance ensures that."

The earl took his rebuke with a calm nod. "Truly, a remarkable philosophy in this age."

Thomas did not tell the earl it was a strategy already over a thousand years old from a far land, a strategy contained in the books of power, hidden far from here, that had enabled him to conquer Magnus.

"Not one soldier died as Magnus fell," Thomas said instead. "That made it much easier to obtain loyalty from a fighting force."

"You have studied warfare?"

"In a certain manner, yes." Thomas also decided it would be wiser to hide that he could read English and Latin—a rare ability, restricted to the higher-ranked priests or monks—and also read and speak the noble's language of French.

"When I arrived," the earl said, "I had not decided what I might do about your new status. I feared I might be forced to waste time by gathering a full force and laying a dreadfully long siege. I have decided against that if you agree to be an ally."

"The answer is yes. And again, I thank you."

"You might not feel that way when you learn more," the earl said heavily.

Thomas raised an eyebrow to frame his question.

"You may remain lord here with my blessing," the earl said, "but I wish to seal with you a loyalty pact."

Thomas hid his joy. A protracted war would not occur!

"That sounds like a reason for celebration, not concern," Thomas said carefully. "You suggested I may not thank you."

The earl pursed his lips. When he spoke, his voice was thick with regret. "I am here to request you go north and defeat the approaching Scots."

Thomas didn't dare blink. To say yes might mean death. To refuse might mean death. He began to formulate a reply.

"Come with me," the earl said, holding up a thick, strong hand to cut Thomas short as he drew a breath. "We shall walk throughout your village."

Thomas, still stunned, managed a weak smile. *At least he calls it* my *village.*

They retraced their steps back through the castle keep, and outside, within minutes, the crowded and hectic action of the village market swallowed them. Pigs squealed. Donkeys brayed. Men shouted. Women shouted. Smells—from the yeasty warmth of baking bread to the pungent filth of emptied chamber pots—swirled around Thomas and the earl.

Despite the push and shove of the crowd, they walked untouched, their rich purple robes as badges of authority. People parted a path in front of them, as water from a ship's bow.

"This battle—"

The earl held a finger to his lips. "Not yet."

They walked.

Through the market. Past the church in the center of the village. Past the collections of whitewashed houses.

Finally, at the base of the ramparts farthest from the keep, the Earl of York slowed his stride.

"Here," he said. He pointed back at the keep. "Walls tend to have ears."

Thomas hoped his face had found calmness by then. "You are asking me to risk my newly acquired lordship by leaving Magnus immediately for battle?"

"You have no one you can trust here in your absence?"

"Can anyone be trusted with such wealth at stake?" Thomas answered.

The earl shrugged. "It is a risk placed upon all of us. I, too, am merely responding to the orders of King Edward II." Darkness crossed his face. "I pray my request need not become an order. Nor an order resisted. Sieges are dreadful matters."

Unexpectedly, Thomas grinned. "That is a well-spoken threat." Thomas continued his grin. "A siege of Magnus, as history has proven, is a dreadful matter for both sides."

"True enough," the earl admitted. He steepled his fingers below his chin. "But Magnus cannot fight forever."

"It needn't fight forever. Just one minute longer than its attackers." The earl laughed again, then became serious.

"This request for help in battle comes for a twofold reason," the earl said. "First, as you know, earldoms are granted and permitted by order of the king of England, Edward II, may he reign long. The power he has granted me lets me in turn hold sway over the lesser earldoms of the north."

A scowl crossed the Earl of York's wide features. "It puts me in a difficult position. Earls who rebel are fools. The king can suffer no traitors. He brings to bear upon them his entire fighting force. Otherwise, further rebellion by others is encouraged. You have—rightly or wrongly—gained power within Magnus. You will keep it as long as you swear loyalty to me, which means loyalty to the king."

Thomas nodded. Sarah, who had given him the plan to conquer Magnus, had anticipated this and explained. But did loyalty include joining forces with one who carried the strange symbol?

Once again, Thomas forced himself to stay in the conversation instead of dwelling upon the earl's ring. After all, the man in front of him was not asking for allegiance to the symbol, but to the king of England.

"Loyalty, of course, dictates tribute be rendered to you," Thomas said.

"Both goods and military support when needed, which I in turn pledge to King Edward," the earl said. "Magnus is yours; that I have already promised. Your price to me is my price to the king. We both must join King Edward in his fight against the Scots."

Thomas knew barely thirty years had passed since King Edward's father had defeated the stubborn tribal Welsh in their rugged hills to the south and west. The Scots to the north, however, had proven more difficult—a task given to Edward II on his father's death. Robert the Bruce led the Scots, whose counterattacks grew increasingly devastating to the English.

Reasons for battle were convincing, as the earl quickly outlined. "If we do not stop this march by our northern enemies, England may have a new Scottish monarch—one who will choose from among his supporters many new earls to fill the English estates. Including ours."

Thomas nodded to show understanding. Yet behind that nod, a single thought continued to transfix him. The symbol. It belonged to an unseen, unknown enemy. One the prisoner in the dungeon refused to reveal.

"Couriers have brought news of a gathering of Scots," the earl explained. "Their main army will go southward on a path near the eastern coast. That army is not our responsibility. A smaller army, however, wishes to take the strategic North Sea castle at Scarborough, only thirty miles from here. I have been ordered to stop it at all costs."

Thomas thought quickly, remembering what Sarah had explained of the North York moors and its geography. "Much better to stop them before they reach the cliffs along the sea."

The earl's eyes widened briefly in surprise. "Yes. A battle along the lowland plains north of here."

"However—"

"There can be no 'however,'" the earl interrupted.

Thomas could match the earl in coldness. "However," he repeated, flint-toned, "you must consider my position. What guarantee do I have this is not merely a ploy to get my army away from this fortress, where we are vulnerable to your attack?"

The earl sighed. "I thought you might consider that. As is custom, I will leave in Magnus a son as hostage. I have no need of more wealth, and his life is worth more than twenty earldoms. Keep him here to be killed at the first sign of my treachery."

Thomas closed his eyes briefly in relief. The earl was not lying then.

Uncontested by reigning royalty, and given officially by charter, Magnus would now remain his. If he survived the battle against the Scots. If he survived the mystery behind the symbol on the ring.

Six

B y this time tomorrow, I will be committed to war.

The Earl of York had departed with his twenty men to the main battle camp—a half-day's ride east—to a valley adjoining the territory of Magnus. Thomas now paced in the privacy of his room of slumber on the highest floor of the castle keep.

Every morning for seven years, Thomas had woken to one thought: conquer Magnus. Before her death, his mother had given him the knowledge to conquer the mighty kingdom. And a reason to do it.

Every night for seven years, the same thought had been his last before entering sleep: conquer Magnus.

War. Again.

Unlike the earlier battle for Magnus, it would be impossible to succeed without a single loss of life. *Will I be numbered among the dead? Or alive, will I see through the mist that seems to surround the strange symbol of evil that the Earl of York wears on a ring of gold?*

The Scots, perhaps, would be an easier enemy to conquer than others hidden in the kingdom itself. Thomas clenched his jaw with new determination. One answer, he suddenly realized, might wait for him in the dungeon.

"Our prisoner fares well?" Thomas asked the soldier guarding the dank passageway to the cells.

"As well as can be expected. As ordered, each day he is granted an hour of sunshine. But he speaks to no one." The guard's voice held faint disapproval at such kind treatment.

Thomas knew a proper lord would discipline a guard who, even in tone, questioned orders. But Thomas smiled instead. "Tell me, I pray, who is crueler? The oppressor, or the oppressed people who, when finally free, punish the oppressor with equal cruelty?"

The guard blinked, the movement barely seen in the dim light of smoky torches. "The oppressor, my lord. 'Tis plain to see."

"Is it plain?" Thoughtfulness softened Thomas's voice. "The oppressor, cruel as he may be, cannot feel the effects of his methods. The oppressed, however, know full well the pain of cruelty. To give the same in return, knowing its evilness, strikes me as the crueler conduct."

Slow understanding crossed the guard's face. "Your own time in the dungeon, my lord, gives you this wisdom?"

"Yes," Thomas said. "You will continue, of course, to ensure a fresh bedding of straw each day?"

"Certainly, my lord." This time the guard's voice reflected full approval.

Thomas waited for his eyes to adjust to the hazy torchlight beyond the guard. He then continued behind the guard through the narrow passageway.

The same rustling of bold rats, the same feeling of cold air that clung damply. Thomas hated the dungeon, hated that he had need to use it.

There were four cells with iron-barred doors. Another guard stood outside the only occupied room, containing the sole prisoner of Magnus, the candle maker who had attacked Isabelle to stop her from uttering secrets that Thomas wanted so badly.

Isabelle. Who had died in front of his eyes. Yet had appeared in his bedchamber as if by magic.

"I wish to see the candle maker," he told the guard.

The clanking of keys, and the screech of a wooden door protesting on ancient hinges.

"Wait outside," Thomas said to the guards as he stepped into the cell. He felt the same despair he did each day as he faced the prisoner there. So much to know, so little given.

The prisoner was a sharp reminder of the dawns that Thomas faced alone when he rose to take what little peace he could find in the early hours, when the wind had yet to rise on the moors and the cry of birds carried from far across the lake surrounding Magnus. It was the time of day when Thomas wondered about the prisoner and searched what answers he'd given for any clues to the secret of Magnus. Now, inside the candle maker's cell, Thomas took stock of his queries and wondered which ones the prisoner might be able to answer.

An old man once cast the sun into darkness and directed me here from the gallows where a knight was about to die, falsely accused. The old man knew Isabelle was a spy. The old man knew my dream of conquering Magnus. Who was that old man? How did he know? Will he ever reappear?

A valiant and scarred knight befriended me and helped me win the castle that once belonged to his own lord. Then departed. Why? Did he do so at the request of the old man?

A crooked candle maker remains in the dungeons of Magnus, refusing to speak, held here because of his need to silence Isabelle. What conspiracy was she about to reveal?

And what fate has fallen upon dear Katherine? How is she able to survive, she with her horribly scarred face hidden behind bandages and whose heart of goodness helped me win Magnus? Who will help her, care for her?

And my books, filled with priceless knowledge, able to give a young man the power to conquer kingdoms. How will I bring them safely to the castle?

And what is the secret of Magnus?

The man who might know, Geoffrey the candle maker, now sat against the far wall, chained to the rough stone blocks. He was a tiny man, with little rounded shoulders and a wrinkled, compact face. He grinned in mockery at his visitor.

Thomas did not waste a moment in greeting. "Answer truth, and you shall be free to leave this cell."

The mocking grin only became wider.

Thomas began his usual questions. "Why did you and the girl Isabelle share the strange symbol?"

The usual reply. Nothing.

"She spoke of a conspiracy before you attempted to stop her through death," Thomas continued. He was not going to tell the prisoner about his midnight visit from Isabelle, real or not. "Who conspires and what hold do they have upon you to keep you in silence?"

Only the dripping of condensed water from the ceiling broke the silence that always followed a question from Thomas.

"Your answers no longer matter," Thomas shrugged. "Just today, I have pledged loyalty to the Earl of York."

Thomas watched the prisoner carefully to see how the news affected him.

Geoffrey laughed. Thomas had not expected that. Yet a reaction to give hope. Either the Earl of York did not belong to those who held the symbol, or the candle maker excelled as an actor.

"The earl has as little hope as do you when already the forces of darkness gather to reconquer Magnus," Geoffrey snorted. "You are fools to think Magnus will not return to—" The candle maker snapped his mouth shut.

"To…?" Thomas pressed. It was as much progress as he had made since capturing Magnus.

That mocking grin shone again in the flickering light.

"To those of the symbol," Geoffrey said flatly. "You shall be long dead by their hands, however, before those behind it are revealed to the world."

SEVEN

T homas stood at the rear of the cathedral in the center of Magnus. Late-afternoon sun warmed the stone floor and etched shadows into the depths of the curved stone ceiling above.

Once, during the anguish of doubt and uncertainty shortly after he'd conquered Magnus, Thomas had finally broken a vow to reject God and the men who served Him. That morning, he had entered the church and found a man who could hear and answer his questions. The questions Thomas had asked that morning, and the answers that been had provided in return, proved a strange but enjoyable beginning for a friendship. Thomas had made it a habit to return frequently for companionship and wisdom.

He waited until the man approached near enough to hear him speak softly.

"I leave tomorrow," Thomas told the man. "I wish to bid you farewell."

The gray-haired elderly man leaned against his broom. "Yes. I have heard. You will lead the men of Magnus into battle against the Scots."

"The procession leaves at dawn—" Thomas stopped himself, then blurted, "How is it you knew?"

Gervaise laughed. Deep and rich. His voice matched the strong lines of humor that marked his old skin. His eyes, however, had prompted Thomas to immediately trust the man at their first meeting.

They held nothing of the greed too often seen in priests and monks who took advantage of their power among superstitious peasants, fearful of God's wrath.

"Thomas, you should not be amazed to discover that men find it crucial to put their souls in order before any battle. I have seen a great number enter the church today for confessions. Many of whom I haven't seen in months."

Not for the first time did Thomas wonder at the wisdom of the older man, who served instead of seeking servants.

"Again the disbelief," he chided with a wry smile, mistaking Thomas's amazement for doubt. "Simple as these men may be at times, they have the wisdom to acknowledge our heavenly Father. Someday, Thomas, the angels will much rejoice to welcome you to the fold."

"Ah, but you well know I am not convinced there are angels."

The smile curved farther upward in response. "Despite the legend you so aptly fulfilled the night you conquered Magnus?"

"Gervaise..."

"'Delivered on the wings of an angel, he shall free us from oppression!' I shall never forget the power of that chant, Thomas. The entire population gathered beneath torchlight by the instructions of a single knight. The appearance of a miracle on white angel wings. Yet you yourself doubt angels?"

"Gervaise!" Thomas tried to inject anger into his voice. And failed.

"Tomorrow you'll be gone, Thomas. Have you any other miracles to astound the Scots?"

"Gervaise! Are you suggesting I arranged the miracle of angel wings?"

"Of course. Our heavenly Father has no need to stoop to such garish dramatics."

Thomas sighed. "You would be kind to keep that belief to yourself. As it is, I am able to hold much sway over the rest of Magnus despite my youth. Leaving this soon would be much less safe for me were it otherwise. I do want to be welcomed back as rightful lord."

"Rightful lord? This is indeed news. Has it to do with a certain visitor who entered Magnus earlier in the day?"

"Little escapes you," Thomas commented, then explained much of his conversation with the earl. But Thomas did not mention the symbol, or his fear of it. Some secrets could not yet be shared.

Gervaise listened carefully. When Thomas finished, the elderly man spoke with simple grace. "And what of your prisoner, my friend? Has Geoffrey revealed why he bludgeoned the former lord's daughter?"

Thomas shook his head. He could not escape the ache that hit him when he was reminded of what he had once felt for Isabelle, and how searing her betrayal had been. Would he see her again?

"Time will answer all," Gervaise said. "It was kind of you to visit during a day that demands many preparations."

"I could not have done otherwise," Thomas replied. The truth in his words surprised him.

Gervaise walked with Thomas to the cathedral doors. "I shall continue praying for you, Thomas. I will rejoice with all of heaven when you accept His most holy presence in your life."

EIGHT

With thick gray hair obscuring most of her face, Katherine leaned upon her cane beside a large wooden frame covered with dried herbs and flowers.

A young woman, belly swollen with child, had asked her a question. But Katherine's attention was on the crowd behind the woman. Among those who filled the market, she spotted Thomas, flanked by a two guards.

Katherine glanced sideways to see if Hawkwood, disguised as an old man beside her, had noticed.

The pregnant woman tapped Katherine on the shoulder.

"Didn't you hear me?" the woman said. "It's my head that hurts. You've got something for me, surely."

"Bark of white willow," Hawkwood answered, handing her a few strands of it. "Boil it, eat the skin, and drink the water."

"Hot or cold?" the pregnant woman asked.

Katherine noticed that Hawkwood had also turned his attention to Thomas. He must have been thinking the same thing. For a day and a half, Thomas had disappeared from the eyes of those who reported to them. And this following the visit from the Earl of York, when all had heard that Thomas was committed to join battle against the Scots. Thomas had been nowhere at all in Magnus, and none had seen him depart. It was almost as if Thomas knew Magnus was riddled with spies.

And now Thomas was back. From where?

"Hot or cold?" the pregnant woman repeated.

"Drink it lukewarm," Hawkwood answered· in his practiced scratchy and feeble voice.

"Laurel," the pregnant woman said. "I need laurel. Seven berries."

When neither answered, she repeated this too. "Laurel berries."

Katherine answered. "Save your coin. It's not true. Seven berries won't prevent labor pains."

"How many then?" she asked, touching her belly.

"John's wort might help," Katherine said, "but nothing will prevent labor pains unless you take something that addles your own wits. But then the babe will be harmed."

"Seven berries," the woman said firmly. "Everyone knows."

Katherine shrugged. Hawkwood had trained her well as an herbalist. She preferred to sell only what was effective, not what was believed to be effective. But peasants clung to superstition, and seven laurel berries, at least, would not hurt the woman or her child.

"What about something to help with hearing?" the woman asked. "Anything for that?"

"You're losing your hearing?" Hawkwood asked.

"Not at all," she said. "It's something both of you need to worry about."

The old man chuckled benevolently and took the woman's coin.

The pregnant woman waddled away, leaving Katherine to move close to Hawkwood. Like hers, Hawkwood's age was an illusion, accomplished with wigs artfully constructed from real hair, long and wild and deliberately filthy. Dirt and soot on their faces and hands helped hide smooth skin. But none would look closely anyway. The bulk of the illusion was accomplished with body language, clothing, and voice.

To the inhabitants of Magnus, the two of them were the ancient couple sent to the market from a monastery in a neighboring valley to dispense medical advice and herbs.

Magnus had a barber, of course, to pull teeth and do surgeries and bloodletting. But the local barber, like all barbers, was to be avoided when possible, unless it was for a simple haircut. Barbers were not known for their delicate touch when pulling teeth or stitching wounds.

Instead, people preferred medicinal plants and roots and herbs, as much less pain was involved in the cure or attempted cure.

Posing as elderly herbalists from outside of Magnus allowed them to come and go as they pleased; since they didn't live in the village, questions were never asked or rumors started when they were gone.

Better yet, as Hawkwood had explained to Katherine, since no one really cared about the lives of the elderly man and woman who served Magnus as herbalists, the roles could be filled if necessary by anyone willing to don a disguise.

For now, Katherine played the role of the old woman herbalist, fully aware that Thomas had put out a reward for anyone who could lead him to her. But Thomas—and all of Magnus—was looking for someone whose face was wrapped in bandages, to hide the scars from a fire.

"I think he intends to come to us," Hawkwood said softly. "Don't look away as if you don't notice. That would be unnatural. He's the lord of Magnus. What's natural is to be watching him closely, like everyone in the market."

This was natural. Lives and livelihoods depended solely on the lord. A good lord dispensed justice without favor. He ensured predictability and comfort for all, from the coarsest of peasants and farm workers to the reeve, marshal, and chancellor. On the other hand, an ill-tempered lord meant misery. Constant fighting with neighboring lords took its toll on the resources of food and weapons and caused disruptions in daily life.

Katherine followed Hawkwood's advice, leaning on the cane as she surveyed his approach.

It wasn't just that he was handsome—for he certainly was—but there was something dignified in his manner, a quiet confidence that spoke far louder than any boisterous swagger. The people of Magnus had begun to fully trust in this new lord, and they treated him with respect as he walked through the crowd, stepping aside and bowing in deference, not fear.

Katherine, too, trusted in the inherent goodness of Thomas; she often revisited the memory of when he had angrily stepped in to protect her from Geoffrey, the candle maker she had once served as if a slave. To Thomas, a stranger, she could have been seen as nothing more than a chattel with a face bound in bandages. Worthless to the rest of the world. But he had defended her as if she were a lady of the court.

A friendship had grown from there, and she'd helped him in conquering Magnus. But Hawkwood had given instructions that she must disappear from his life, so she had, hoping someday it might be different between them.

As Thomas reached the stall with the wood frame of herbs behind them, his guards stepped away, leaving him privacy to address Katherine and Hawkwood.

"I would like yarrow," Thomas said, pointing at the bunches of dried stalks with small clusters of yellow at the top. He spoke with a coldness that seemed at odds with the Thomas she had spent hours with in conversation. Had power changed him already? "All that you have."

Yarrow. To heal wounds and cure infections. Thomas must be looking ahead to the needs that would follow battle against the Scots.

Hawkwood turned to take the bunches of dried yarrow from the wood frame, but Thomas stopped him with another question.

"And seeds of henbane. Your poppy and mandrake, as well."

Hawkwood turned back and spoke to Thomas, hardly above a quiet whisper. "Is there someone you intend to bewitch?"

NINE

I s there someone you intend to bewitch?"

Thomas didn't answer, as something scratched at his side.

He reached beneath his cloak for a tiny cage hanging from a loop of leather belted around his waist.

With practiced movements of his fingers, he unlatched the cage without looking at it.

The fact that he had a small cage on his body was not unusual. Fleas were a common nuisance. Women often wore a patch of fur near the neck to attract the fleas and keep them off their skin and out of their hair. Others resorted to a small cage with a piece of suet where roaming fleas would get stuck.

A few days earlier, a local craftsman had built a slightly larger cage, and for Thomas, it held not suet, but a tame blind white mouse.

He opened the cage door, and the mouse scooted onto his palm. Thomas lifted the mouse into the open and stroked its head with his index finger. He used his other hand to find grain in a side pocket.

He gave a seed to the mouse. It perched and nibbled at the seed as Thomas answered the old man's question.

"My intentions are no concern of yours," Thomas said. He kept his voice cold. For all he knew, an enemy stood in front of him. "I am not here to answer your questions, but you will answer mine."

"Of course, my lord," the old man said, bowing and stepping slightly back.

"First," Thomas said, "have you seeds of henbane?"

Henbane. Grind the seeds into powder, apply the powder with an ointment rubbed onto a man's forearm. Hallucinations and visions would follow.

Thomas knew this not because he was a witch or an herbalist himself, but because of where he'd been over the last two days—on a trip of solitude. Well hidden from Magnus, and known only to him, was a small cache of a collection of books that had been his legacy, books of priceless knowledge.

He'd used a portion of his time with the books to study the sections that dealt with medicinal plants and roots and herbs, confirming his suspicions about the night of his visitation by Isabelle.

Because the guards had rushed in to find him alone, he'd dismissed them, telling them he must have cried out in his sleep. Then in his books he had discovered the reason for the sensation of a giant hand gripping his body. With only one explanation for how someone had done this without wakening him, he'd tested it by setting aside the remains of his evening meal, half finished on a plate in his bedchamber, and feeding a small portion of it to a mouse the next morning.

When the mouse had fallen asleep on the plate, and didn't even stir when prodded with the point of a knife, the conclusion was beyond doubt; he'd been drugged. He suspected henbane because of the dreams and his slowed reactions during his conversation with Isabelle.

Her presence, however, could not have been all hallucination.

Which had led Thomas to other questions that had no answers. Who had drugged him? How had Isabelle entered the room? How had she then disappeared so quickly while the explosion blinded him?

"My lord," the old man answered as he swept his arms to indicate the herbs and roots hanging behind him, "of henbane, we have none."

"I am willing to pay a month's wages for a mere handful," Thomas said. "How long will it take for you to acquire it?"

Thomas watched closely, hoping for a greedy reply. He was disappointed when the old man shrugged and shook his head against it.

"For even a year's wages, I cannot find you henbane."

"Poppy and mandrake?" Thomas asked.

"I could enquire at the monastery, but I'm sure there will be none."

If the old herbalist was lying, Thomas could gain nothing by asking more questions. If he truly had no knowledge, then this old man would not be able to lead Thomas to anyone who might have drugged him.

"Ah yes," Thomas said. His time had not been entirely wasted, for he had another purpose for stopping at this stall in the market. "I understand you are sent here weekly from the monastery."

"As you well know, Magnus is not open to allowing a monastery," the old man answered. "Yet there is need among your people for what the gardens provide."

By tradition, monks were the ones with the knowledge of how to grow the medicinal plants and herbs.

"You are a monk?" Thomas asked.

"No. But the monastery provides for us."

Thomas glanced at the old woman. "Does she speak?"

"Yes, my lord," the old woman croaked.

"Good," Thomas said. "As you may have heard, allegiance to the Earl of York requires that I raise an army to join him in battle against the Scots. Magnus does not have its own herbalist, and I will require one to accompany my army on the march. Since I expect the monks will not be willing to let both of you depart for an uncertain amount of time, I only ask that one of you gives service."

"But, my lord—"

Thomas did not give the old man a chance to finish. "This is not a request, but a demand. Your monks are shrewd enough to realize that they do not want to make an enemy of me. I need barbers to tend to my men, but just as importantly, an herbalist. Willingly, or as prisoner, one of you will remain here to become part of the march. Decide who stays and who returns to the monks."

The old man and the old woman exchanged glances. The old man, as Thomas expected, was the one to make the decision.

"You will take her," he said.

The old woman seemed to shake slightly as she leaned on her cane and bowed her head.

"Fear not," Thomas told her. "You will be far behind the battle lines, and I will make sure that no harm comes to you."

Ten

A council of war had been called. Gathered in a small circle beneath the shade of a towering oak stood fourteen of the most powerful earls and barons in the north of England. Among them, Thomas.

"David, will you permit a snot-nosed boy to remain with us in council?" The questioner, a fat middle-aged man whose chubby fingers were studded with massive gold rings, did not hide his contempt and surprise to see Thomas.

"Aye, Frederick, the lord of Magnus remains," replied the Earl of York.

"But these are matters of war!" exploded the fat man, spraying spittle on those nearest him.

Some nodded agreement. Others waited for the Earl of York to respond again. All stared at Thomas.

The fat man yelled to repeat his challenge. "These are matters of war!"

Part of his mind noted the festive hum beyond the circle of barons, but despite the malice of the fat man in front of Thomas, another part of his thoughts also held sadness. *Before the army's return, many men will die, to leave behind widows or orphans.*

Thinking of the lives that faced destruction and determined to ensure as few died as possible in the upcoming days, Thomas surveyed the other men in the circle. His only friend—if someone carrying the symbol could be a friend—might be the Earl of York.

Show no fear. Lose respect here and your own men will never follow. Lose your men, and you lose control of Magnus.

Thomas fought the impulse to lick his suddenly dry lips. If the Earl of York did not vouch for him, he would be forced to prove himself immediately. A fight, perhaps. These were solid, grown men who had scrabbled for power on the strength of steel nerves and iron willpower. Would Robert of Uleran's training be enough for him to survive a fight here and now?

The Earl of York delayed the answer to that question by replying with the quietness of authority. "Frederick, this 'snot-nose' you so casually address had the intelligence to conquer the ultimate fortress, Magnus. Could you have done the same, even with an army of a thousand? Could you have done it without the loss of a single life and managed to obtain the loyalty and gratitude of its people?"

That brought respectful silence from all of them.

The Earl of York laughed to break the discomfort of his rebuke. "Besides, Frederick, this 'boy' is already taller than you. When he fills to match the size of his hands, he'll be a terrible enemy. Treat him well while you can."

The others joined in the laughter.

Thomas realized that if this meeting were to end now, he would simply be regarded as a special pet favored by the Earl of York. Yet could he risk the earl's anger?

The laughter continued.

"I need no special treatment," Thomas suddenly declared, then felt the thud of his heart in the immediate silence.

Was it too early to reveal the weapons his men had practiced in secrecy?

Thomas hoped the narrowing of the Earl of York's eyes meant curiosity, not anger at the insult of publicly casting aside his approval.

You've gone too far to turn back.

"Tomorrow, when we rest at midday from the march," Thomas said, "I propose a contest."

ELEVEN

S leep came upon Thomas quickly that night.

He dreamed of his mother, who had taught him through his childhood, had given him the quest of conquering Magnus, and had prepared him for an earldom before dying of the pox.

He dreamed of Katherine, dirty bandages around the horribly scarred flesh of her face, and how she, at the end, had made it possible for him to conquer Magnus.

And slowly, he woke to perfume and the softness of hair falling across his face. *Isabelle? Again?*

He drew breath to challenge the intruder, but a light finger across his lips and a gentle shushing stopped him from speaking.

"Dress quickly, Thomas. Follow without protest," the voice whispered.

Thomas saw only the darkness of silhouette in the dimness of the tent.

Could this be Isabelle?

"You've returned," Thomas said.

"Returned? There is no time for your riddles and nonsense."

"Then who are you?" Thomas reached for his sword, a movement that the intruder must have noticed, even in the darkness.

"Fear not," the voice continued. "You don't need to defend yourself. An old man wishes to see you. He asks if you remember the gallows."

Old man! Gallows! In a rush of memory as bright as daylight, Thomas felt himself at the gallows. The knight who might win Magnus for him about to be hung, and Thomas in front, attempting a rescue through disguise and trickery. Then the arrival of an old man, one who knew it was Thomas behind the disguise and knew of his quest, one who commanded the sun into darkness. One who had never appeared again.

"As you wish," Thomas whispered in return with as much dignity as he could muster, despite the sudden trembling in his stomach. No mystery—not even the evil terror of the strange symbol—was more important to him than discovering the old man's identity.

The silhouette backed away slowly, beckoning Thomas with a single crooked finger. He rose quickly, wrapped his cloak around him, and shuffled into his shoes.

How had she avoided the sentries outside his tent?

Thomas pushed aside the flap of the tent and followed. Her perfume hung in the heavy night air.

Moonlight showed that both sentries sat crookedly against the base of a nearby tree. Asleep! It was within his rights as lord to have them executed.

"Forgive them," the voice whispered as if reading his mind. "Their suppers contained potions of drowsiness."

He strained to see the face of the silhouette in the light of the large pale moon. In response, she pulled the flaps of her hood across her face. All he saw was a tall and slender figure, leading him slowly along a trail that avoided all tents and campsites.

Ghost-white snakes of mist hung heavy among the solitary trees of the moor valley.

It felt too much like a dream to Thomas. Still, he did not fear to follow. Only one person had knowledge of what had transpired in front of the gallows. Only he, then, could have sent the silhouette to his tent.

At the farthest edge of the camp, she stopped to turn and wait.

When Thomas arrived, she took his right hand and clasped it with her left.

"Who are you?" Thomas asked. "Show me your face."

"Hush, Thomas," she whispered.

"You know my name. You know my face. Yet you hide from me."

"Hush," she repeated.

"No," he said with determination. "Not a step farther will I take. The old man wishes to see me badly enough to drug my sentries. He will be angry if you do not succeed in your mission."

She did not answer. Instead, she lifted her free hand slowly, pulled the hood from her face, and shook her hair loose to her shoulders.

Nothing in his life had prepared him for that moment.

The sudden ache of joy to see her face hit him like a blow. For a timeless moment, it took from him all breath. He had never seen this woman before, but somehow, deep in his soul, it seemed as if he had known her his entire life.

It was not her beauty that brought him such joy, even though the curved shadows of her face would be forever seared in his mind. No. Thomas had learned not to trust appearances; beauty consisted of heart joining heart, not eyes to eyes. Isabelle, somewhere lurking within Magnus, had used her exquisite features to deceive, while gentle Katherine—horribly burned and masked by bandages—had proven the true worth of friendship.

Thomas struggled for composure. What, then, drew him to this woman? Why did it seem as if he had been long-pledged for this very moment?

She stared back, as if knowing completely how he felt, yet fearless of what was passing between them.

"Your name," Thomas said. "What is your name?"

"I don't have a name."

"Everyone has a name."

"Everyone of this world," she answered. "What if I am nothing more than a spirit? A walking dream?"

"You toy with me. As if you already know me. Who are you?"

"Someone who wants to believe that you are one of us," she answered.

"One of you? A spirit? A walking dream?"

As answer, she took his hand, lifted it to her mouth, and kissed the back of his hand so gently that he wondered if he had imagined her lips brushing against his skin.

She dropped his hand again. "I have already said too much. Follow me. The old man wishes to see you."

Abruptly, she turned, and he had no choice but to follow as she picked faultless footsteps on ground shadowed from the moon by the trees along the stream of the valley.

Thomas bit his lip to keep inside a cry of emotion he could barely comprehend. Isabelle's betrayal at Magnus now seemed a childish pain. He drew dignity around him like armor.

They walked—it could have been only a heartbeat, he felt so distant from the movement of time—until reaching a hill that rose steeply into the black of the night.

An owl called.

She turned to the sound and walked directly into the side of the hill. As if parting the solid rock by magic, she slipped sideways into an invisible cleft between monstrous boulders. Thomas followed.

They stood completely surrounded by the granite walls of a cave long hollowed smooth by eons of rainwater. The air seemed to press down upon him and away from the light of the moon; Thomas saw only velvet black.

He heard the returning call of an owl leave her lips, and before he could react to the noise, there was a small spark. His eyes adjusted to see an old man holding the small light of a torch, which grew as the pitch caught fire.

Light gradually licked upward around them to reveal a bent old man, wrapped in a shawl. Thomas could distinguish no features beyond deep wrinkles. Shadows leaped and danced in eerie circles from beneath his chin.

"Greetings, Thomas of Magnus." The voice was a slow whisper. "Congratulations on succeeding in your first task, the conquering of the castle."

"My first task? Who are you?"

"Such impatience. One who is lord of Magnus would do well to temper his words among strangers."

"I will not apologize," Thomas said, filled with indignation. "Each day I am haunted by memory of you. Impossible that you should know my quest at the hanging. Impossible that the sun should fail that morning at your command."

The old man shrugged and continued in the same strained whisper. "Impossible is often merely a perception. Surely by now you have been able to ascertain the darkness was no sorcery, but merely a trick of astronomy as the moon moves past the sun. Your books would inform a careful reader that such eclipses may be predicted."

"What do you know of my books?"

That mystery gripped Thomas so tightly he could almost forget the presence of the other in the cave. The young woman.

The old man ignored the urgency in Thomas's words. "My message is the same as when we last spoke after the gallows. You must bring the winds of light into this age and resist the forces of darkness poised to take from you the kingdom of Magnus. Yet what assistance I may offer is little. The decisions to be made are yours."

Thomas clenched his fists and in frustration exhaled a blast of air. "You talk in circles. Tell me who you are. Tell me clearly what you want of me. And tell me the secret of Magnus."

The old man turned away from Thomas, disappearing and reappearing in the shadows of the cave.

"Druids, Thomas. Beware those barbarians from the isle. They will attempt to conquer you through force. Or through bribery."

Yet another layer of cryptic answers. "Tell me how you knew of my quest that day at the hanging. Tell me how you know of the books. Tell me how you know of the barbarians."

"To tell you is to risk all."

Thomas pounded his thigh in anger. "The risk is shrouded and hidden from me. I am given a task that is unexplained, with no reason to fulfill it beyond my vow to my mother. And then you imply it is but the first of more tasks. Give me answers. No more circles!"

Even in his frustration, Thomas sensed sadness from the old man.

"The knowledge you already have is worth the world, Thomas. Use it wisely to save your own men from the Scots. That is all I can say in that regard."

"No," Thomas pleaded. "Who belongs to the strange symbol of conspiracy? Is the Earl of York friend or enemy?"

The old man shook his head. "Thomas, I pray there will come a day when we can trust you and reveal your destiny."

"We? At least tell me who you are!"

"Thomas, give us a reason to trust. Very soon, you will be offered a prize that will seem far greater than the kingdom of Magnus."

The torch flared once before dying, and Thomas read deep concern in the old man's eyes.

From the sudden darkness came his final whispered words. "It is worth your soul to refuse."

TWELVE

Dawn broke clear and bright. Despite the cold that resulted from a cloudless night, few complained. Rain would be churned into a sucking mud beneath the thousands of feet of an army this size. White mist, common to the moors, would disorient stragglers within minutes. Cold and clear nights, then, were much better for warfare.

Before the sun grew hot, all tents had been dismantled and packed. Then, with much confusion and shouting, the earls and barons directed their men so that the entire army formed an uneven column nearly a half mile in length—so long that the front banners began forward motion nearly twenty minutes before the ones in the rear.

The army marched only for three miles before an eerie noise began.

To Thomas, it sounded like the faraway buzzing of bees. Once he actually lifted his head to search for the cloud of insects. The whispering became a hum, and the hum gradually became a babble. The noise came from the army itself.

Still, the army moved its slow pace forward.

Finally the babble reached Thomas and his men, who were moving in the middle of the mass and slowly making progress to reach the front. Pieces of excited conversation became audible.

"Demons upon us!"

"We are fated to doom!"

"Pray the Lord takes mercy upon us!"

Then, like the quiet eye of an ominous storm, the voices immediately in front died. That sudden calmness chilled Thomas more than the most agitated words that had reached his ears.

Within sixty more paces, he understood the horrified silence.

Thomas felt rooted at the sight, and only the pressure of movement behind him kept him in motion.

To the side of the steady motion of the column stood a small clearing. Facing the column, as if ready to charge, and stuck solidly on iron bars imbedded into the ground, were the massive heads of two white bulls.

Blood—in dried rivulets on the iron bars—had pooled beneath the heads. Flies, gorged on the thick rust-red liquid, swarmed beneath the line of vision of the open yet sightless eyes of each head.

The remains of a huge fire scarred the grass between the heads. Little remained of its fuel, but charred hooves carefully arranged outward in a circle left little doubt that the bodies of the animals had been burned.

Thomas looked upward. Again a chill of the unnatural nearly froze his steps.

At first, it appeared as heavy ribbons hanging from the branches of a nearby tree. Then, as Thomas focused closer, he fought the urge to retch. Pieces of entrails draped over the branches swayed lightly in the wind.

Carved clearly into the trunk of the tree was the strange symbol of conspiracy, the one that matched the ring of the Earl of York.

Thomas closed his eyes in cold fear. Words spat with hatred by Geoffrey echoed through his head.

Already the forces of darkness gather to reconquer Magnus.

Thomas shivered again beneath the hot blue sky.

THIRTEEN

Thomas's bold challenge would take place at noon—in a scant hour. Not for the first time did he doubt its outcome and his own destiny.

Alone with a bowl of stew, he sat on a knoll that gave him a view of much of the camp. From knights and squires and yeomen and archers to cooks and peasants and those who simply followed for merriment, there were hundreds who depended on the choices he made.

Who was he to pretend it was within his capabilities to wisely govern them all? And in the end, was it a good enough reason, simply because his long-dead parents had once ruled Magnus? What would all of his efforts bring him except power that some mysterious conspiracy seemed to continuously try to take?

He felt a scratching in the cage hidden beneath his cloak. The tame mouse smelled food and had learned to expect to be fed.

Thomas let the mouse crawl onto his hand. He'd been reluctant to have the mouse blinded to keep it from escaping, for he hated any act of cruelty. But better to risk the life of a mouse than that of an official food taster. The mouse, at least, was content. Not so much for the man who would sample every meal, wondering not only if it might be his last taste, but the beginning of a horrible and painful death by poison.

Thomas placed the mouse on his shoulder. He felt the twitching whiskers against his neck.

With both hands free, he slid some stew onto the flat of his knife blade. He set the bowl down with one hand, and kept the knife steady with his other. Then he reached across and gently lifted the mouse off his shoulder and onto his other wrist. The mouse crept forward and with delicate movements scooped the juices of the stew into its mouth.

Thomas's thoughts drifted away from the mouse, back to the hidden library that he'd consulted before this march. He'd found advice on herbs and medicinal plants. He'd made military plans based on other portions of the books. But nothing in any of the books had prepared him for battle against those of the strange symbol.

Why not? he wondered. Why had his own mother not spoken a single word about Druids? Surely, on her deathbed when she'd made him pledge to reconquer Magnus, she could have anticipated that those who ruled it were masters of apparent darkness?

A slight movement distracted Thomas. He glanced down at his wrist, where the mouse was staggering in tiny circles. At that moment, it tumbled sideways and landed in the grass. It kicked and shuddered, then stopped.

FOURTEEN

This challenge may be a waste of time," growled Frederick. His jowls wobbled with each word. "But I'm in favor of anything to make these peasants forget the morning's unholy remains."

White bulls, rare and valuable beyond compare, suggested a special power that appealed to even the least superstitious peasants. What demons might be invoked with such a carefully arranged slaughter of the animals?

It was a question asked again and again throughout the morning. Now, with the army at midday rest, nothing else would be discussed.

Thomas felt the pressure. He faced the barons and earls around him. "If each of you would, please summon your strongest and best—"

"Swordsmen?" Frederick sneered. "I'll offer to fight you myself."

"Yeomen," Thomas finished.

"Bah. An archery contest. Where's the blood in that?"

"Precisely," Thomas said. He wondered briefly how the fat man had ever become an earl. "How does it serve our purpose to draw blood among ourselves when the enemy waits to do the same?"

The reply drew scattered laughs. Someone clapped Thomas on the back. "Well spoken!"

The fat man would not be deterred. "What might a few arrows prove? Everyone knows battles are won in the glory of the charge. In the nobility of holding the front line against a countercharge. Man against man. Beast against beast. Bravery against bravery until the enemy flees."

Thomas noticed stirrings of agreement from the other earls and barons. He felt like a puppy among starving dogs. Yet he welcomed the chance to argue a method of warfare that had well served generals two oceans away and nearly two thousand years earlier.

"Man against man? Beast against beast?" Thomas countered as he thought of the books of knowledge that had won him Magnus. "Lives do not matter?"

"We command from safety," Frederick said with smugness. "Our lives matter and are well protected. It has always been done in this manner."

Thomas drew a breath. Was it his imagination, or was the Earl of York, still silent, enjoying this argument? The thought gave him new determination.

"There are better methods," Thomas said quickly. He removed all emotion from his voice, and the flattening of his words drew total attention.

"The bulk of this army—and any other—consists of poorly trained farmers and villagers. None with armor. How they must fear the battle."

"The fear makes them fight harder!" Frederick snorted.

"Knowing they are to be sacrificed like sheep?"

"It has always been done in this manner," Frederick repeated.

"Listen," Thomas said, with urgency. He knew as he spoke that some of the earls were considering his words carefully. If he could present his argument clearly...

"If these men knew you sought to win battles and preserve their lives, loyalty and love would make them far better soldiers than fear of death."

"But—"

Thomas would brook no interruption. "Furthermore, man against man, beast against beast dictates that the largest and strongest army will win."

"Of course. Any simpleton knows that," Frederick said, his voice laced with scorn.

"And if we should find ourselves the lesser army of the two?"

Silence.

Thomas spoke from memory a passage of one of his secret books. "I would suggest an art of using troops in this way: When you have ten to the enemy's one, surround him. When you have five times his strength, attack him. If you only have double his strength, divide the enemy. If you are equally matched to the enemy, when the situation permits, then engage him in battle. If you are weaker in numbers, there is no shame in withdrawing and being prepared and able to do so. Lastly, if in all respects you are unequal to a fight, then elude the enemy."

Thomas noticed slack-jawed mouths in response to his answer. It was an ancient wisdom, but none in front of him, of course, could even guess at the source of it or how Thomas had acquired it.

Thomas continued. "War—all war—is deception. The most important thing in war is to attack the enemy's strategy."

Thomas watched the Earl of York nod in satisfaction at Thomas's words, and so he finished speaking from his memories. "I would suggest most of all that the supreme victory would be to subdue an enemy without fighting."

More silence.

The fat one recovered first and sputtered in an obvious attempt to recover his pride. "Bah. Words. Simply words. What have they to do with an archery contest?"

"There is no point in explaining what you will not believe until you see," Thomas said, "and if you want to see what you might not be able to believe, gather your best archers."

FIFTEEN

The opposing fourteen bowmen lined up first. Each had been chosen for height and strength. Longer arms drew a bowstring back farther, which meant more distance. Stronger arms were steadier, which meant better accuracy.

Seven targets were set two hundred yards away. People packed both sides of the field so that the space to the targets appeared as a wide alley of untrampled grass.

Without fanfare, the first seven of the selected archers fired. Five of the seven arrows pierced completely the leather shields set up as targets. One arrow hit the target and bounced off, but even that was a good enough feat to be acknowledged with brief applause. The other arrow flew barely wide and quivered to a rest in the ground behind the targets.

The results of such fine archery drew gasps, even from a crowd experienced in warfare.

The next seven archers accomplished almost the same. Five more arrows pierced the targets. The other two flew high and beyond. More gasps.

Then Thomas and his men stepped to the firing line.

In direct contrast, Thomas had chosen small men with shorter arms. The obvious dissimilarity drew incredulous murmurs from the crowd.

Thomas stood at the line with his twelve men. He spoke in low tones heard only by them. "You have practiced much. Yet I would prefer that we attempt nothing that alarms you."

He paused and studied them. Each returned his look with a smile. Smiles?

"You enjoy this?" Thomas asked.

They nodded. "We know these weapons well," one said. "Such a demonstration will set men on their ears."

Thomas grinned in relief. "Then I propose this. We will request that the targets be moved back until the first of you says no farther. Thus, none of you will fear the range."

More smile and nods.

Thomas then turned and shouted down the field. "More distance!"

He noted with satisfaction the renewed murmuring from the crowd. The men at the targets stopped ten steps back and began to position them in place.

"Farther!" Thomas commanded.

Louder murmurs. The best archers in an army of thousands had already shot at maximum range!

"Farther!" Thomas shouted when the men with targets paused. Five steps, ten steps, twenty steps. Finally, one of the archers whispered the range was enough. By then, the targets were nearly a quarter of the distance farther than they had been set originally.

The crowd knew such range was impossible. Expectant silence replaced disbelieving murmurs.

Thomas made no person wait.

He dropped his hand, and within seconds a flurry of arrows hissed toward the leather shields.

Few spectators were able to turn their heads quickly enough to follow the arrows.

Eleven arrows thudded solidly home. One arrow drove through the shield completely, spraying stripped feathers in all directions. The final two arrows overshot the targets and landed twenty yards farther down.

Thomas wanted to jump with joy and amazement, as many in the crowd did. To shoot arrows so much farther and so much faster, with so much more power than had ever been witnessed, was almost like magic.

Instead, he turned calmly to his archers and raised his voice to be heard. He smiled. "Survey the crowd and remember this for your grandchildren. It's not often in a lifetime so few are able to set so many on their ears."

Sixteen

Clothed in the dirty and coarse fabric of a peasant woman, Isabelle held a long, slender stick that she had used to herd geese toward a wide patch of grass on a hillside.

All of the geese on the grass below her could have been slaughtered before the march started, but then the meat would have begun to spoil. Instead, although it took much more work than loading plucked and gutted carcasses on a wagon, the army fed itself by taking along live-stock of all sorts, including these geese.

The peasant woman who normally tended to the geese had somewhat unexpectedly sickened before the march—it had been unexpected for her, but not for Isabelle. The dosage of a potion she'd added to the woman's food during the preparations for the march had done its job.

While Isabelle was able to stay close enough to Thomas without drawing attention to herself, she wished she was away from the filthy geese and the constant squawking and honking and the greasy piles of green that she had given up trying to avoid as she walked. But those she served had given her no choice.

She sat on a hillside with a jar of jam and some black bread, ready to eat, when the army's cook ambled over to report after the afternoon meal had been given.

"No, 'twas nothing unusual at all," the cook said. "Except, of course, for the lord of Magnus's archery contest."

"You're telling me that he did nothing after his lunch except host an archery contest?" Isabelle asked the cook. "You gave him the stew?"

"All of it. He went up on a hillside alone as he often does. When he returned, the bowl was empty."

Isabelle frowned. In Magnus, she'd been given instructions. After the discovery of the slain white bulls, ensure that Thomas is seen going temporarily insane. A potion had been carefully mixed with the right combination of herbs and medicinal roots that would give Thomas a far deeper set of hallucinations than on the evening she had visited his bedchamber.

"Does he suspect you?" Isabelle asked the cook.

"He's eaten everything I served him," he said. "At least when I'm watching. I can't speak for his time on the hillside."

How could Thomas know what had been planned against him? What would those who gave her orders say when they learned she had failed? Isabelle had no one with whom to discuss her questions.

It was supposed to be simple. The white bulls would begin rumors among the peasants and the rest of the army camp. Once that was followed by a bout of insanity by Thomas, he would appear cursed, and his leadership would be destroyed. Then he'd be forced to pledge loyalty to those of the symbol in order to keep Magnus.

Instead, Thomas had only strengthened his reputation by the apparent showmanship of the archery contest. The cook went on to describe the magical display put on by Thomas's archers, but Isabelle wasn't fooled. She, too, had been taught how an inner circle of knowledge could be used to appear as magic.

But where had Thomas learned how to make weaponry so much more powerful than anything in England? It was obvious that Thomas held knowledge that the Druids needed to possess. They needed him to pledge his loyalty to them—not only for their gain, but to keep it out of the hands of the enemy. In the bedchamber, her first attempt had failed; she expected something like the slain bulls would be done soon to put more pressure on Thomas, but she was not close enough to those who made the plans to know what it was.

"Where's my silver?" the cook asked. "I've done all that you wanted from me. I want double what you promised. Whatever you wanted me to put into his food didn't affect him. If you don't pay, I'll report to Thomas that you asked me to poison him and refused."

"You think I carry it with me?" she said. "So that thieves such as you can take it all? Tonight I'll bring it, the same way I delivered the potion to you yesterday."

"You have until tonight then. I'm warning you."

"Choose your goose and be done with it," Isabelle said. She took a piece of bread and tilted the jam jar so that it oozed onto the bread, aware of the cook's hungry eyes. There was a reason his belly was the most obvious part of his body. "I'll see you tonight."

"Remember. Double the silver." He made no move toward the geese, and his eyes remained locked on the bread and jam in her hand.

She gave a sigh of exasperation and stood. "It's this that you're wanting too?"

She extended the bread, and he snatched it from her, eating it as he walked the short distance to the geese. He finished the jam and bread before reaching the geese. He took the sack off his shoulder and poured the handful of grain from the bottom of the sack onto the ground, then waited for a silly and greedy goose to push its way toward it. As the goose dropped its head, the cook slipped the sack over it and then pulled the sack upward. The evening meal kicked from inside the sack but was helpless to prevent its fate.

Wasn't that how it went? Isabelle thought. Get silly and greedy, and danger will strike.

As the cook strolled down the hillside, she put away the jam untouched.

She'd never had any intention of eating it—not with the powders that had been mixed into it.

No. The jam had been meant for someone silly and greedy. Someone now helpless to prevent his fate as he walked away with a goose in a sack slung over his shoulder.

SEVENTEEN

She was the oldest woman he could find during a hurried search of the other campsites as the last of dusk quickly settled.

Even in the lowered light, Thomas saw the grease that caked deep wrinkles on her hands and fingers. One of the cooks, no doubt. Part of the army that serves an army.

She sat leaning her back against a stone that jutted from the flattened grass. Her shabby gray cloak did not have a hood, and her hair had thinned enough so that her scalp shone, stretched shiny and tight, in the firelight. A grotesque contrast to the skin that hung in wattles from her cheeks and jaw.

"Ho! Ho!" she cackled as Thomas stopped in front of her. "Have all the young women spurned your company? Tsk. Tsk. And such a handsome devil you are."

She took a gulp from a leather bag. "Come closer, dearie. Share my wine!"

Thomas moved closer, but shook his head. She smelled of many days squatting in front of a cook fire and of many weeks unbathed.

She pulled the wine back and gulped again. Then cocked her head. "You'd be Thomas of Magnus. The young warrior. I remember from the archery contest." Another gulp. "I'll not rise to bow. At my age, there is little I fear. Certainly not the displeasure of an earl." She finished her sentence with a coughing wheeze.

Instinct had told Thomas that the older among them would know the tales he needed, the tales he did not hear the night before.

So he asked. "Druids. Would you fear Druids?"

The old crone clutched her wine bag, then took a slower swallow and gazed thoughtfully at Thomas. From deep within her face, black eyes glittered traces of the nearby campfire.

"Druids? That is a name to be spoken only with great care. Where would someone so young get a name so ancient and so forgotten?"

"The burning of two white bulls," Thomas guessed. He was still working on instinct, and the old man in the cave had not connected Druids with those sights. "A symbol that inspires terror."

"Nay, lad. That's not how you conjured the dreaded name. A host of others in this army have seen the same. Not once have I heard the name of those evil sorcerers cross any lips."

Evil sorcerers!

"So," she continued, "it is not from their rituals you offer that name, although none have guessed so true. Confess, boy. How is it you know what none others perceive?"

He was right, he thought. Druids were behind the symbol. That meant Druids were behind the conspiracy to take Magnus. What might this old, old woman know of their tales?

Thomas did not flinch at her stare. *Keep her speaking,* he commanded himself. He tried to bluff. "Perhaps one merely has knowledge of their usual activities."

The crone revealed her gums in a wide smile. "But of course! You're from Magnus."

Thomas froze and every nerve ending tingled. Magnus. Druids. As if it were natural that there was a connection between the two.

"What," he asked through a tightened jaw, "would such imply?"

"Hah! You do know less than you pretend!" The crone patted the ground beside her. "Come. Sit. Listen to what my own grandmother once told me."

Slowly, Thomas moved beside her. A bony hand clutched his knee.

"There have been over a hundred winters since she was a young girl," the old crone said of her grandmother. "When she told me these tales, she had become as old then as I am now. Generations have come and died since her youth then and my old age now. In that time, common knowledge of those ancient sorcerers has disappeared. Even in my grandmother's youth, she told me, Druids were rarely spoken of. And now…" The crone shrugged. "Yet you come now with questions." The bony hand squeezed his leg and she asked abruptly. "Do you seek their black magic?"

"It is the furthest thing from my desires."

"I hear truth in your words, boy. Let me, then, continue."

Thomas waited. So close to answers, it did not matter how badly she smelled. His heart thudded, and for a moment, he wondered if she heard.

Then she began again. Her breath washed over Thomas, hot and oddly sweet from wine. "*Druid* means 'Finder of the Oak Tree.' It is where they gather, deep in the forests, to begin their rituals. I was told that their circle of high priests and sorcery began long ago in the mists of time, on the isle of the Celts. They study philosophy, astronomy, and the lore of the gods."

Astronomy! The old man in the cave had known enough astronomy to predict the eclipse of the sun!

Thomas stood and paced, then realized her voice had stopped.

"I'm sorry," he said. "Please, please continue."

"They also offer human sacrifices for the sick or for those in danger of death in battle." The crone crossed herself and after that, swallowed more wine. "I remember the fear in my grandmother's eyes as she told me. And the legends still persist. Whispers among the very old. It is said that when the Romans overran our island—before the time of the Saxons and before the time of the Viking raiders—they forced the Druids to accept Christianity. But that was merely appearance. Through the hundreds of years, the circle of high priests held on to their knowledge of the ways of evil. Once openly powerful, now they remain hidden."

Thomas could not contain himself longer. "Magnus!" he said. "You spoke of Magnus."

Her hand clutched his knee one final time, then relaxed. From her came a soft laugh. "Bring me a feast tomorrow. Rich meat. Cheese. Buttered bread. And much wine. That is my price for the telling of ancient tales."

After a cackle of glee, she dropped her head to her chest and soon began to snore.

Then, without warning, the snoring ceased and she lifted her head.

"There is one other who knows more than I. She is the herbalist who visits Magnus weekly. Perhaps when you return to the castle, you can ask her."

Then the woman began to snore again, obviously unaware that Thomas had ordered the herbalist to march with his army.

EIGHTEEN

The northward march began again. Memory of the slaughter of two white bulls faded quickly, it seemed, and all tongues spoke only of the archery contest.

Thomas and his men had little time to enjoy their sudden fame, however. Barely an hour later, the column of people slowed, then stopped.

Low grumbling rose. Some strained to see ahead, hoping to find reason for the delay. Others—older and wiser—flopped themselves into the shade beneath trees and sought sleep.

Thomas, on horseback near his men, saw the runner approaching from a long distance ahead. As he neared, Thomas saw the man's eyes rolling white with exhaustion.

"Sire!" he stumbled and panted. "The Earl of York wishes you to join him at the front!"

"Do you need to reach more commanders down the line?" Thomas asked.

The man heaved for breath, and could only nod.

Thomas nodded at a boy beside him. "Take this man's message," he instructed. "Please relay it to the others and give him rest."

With that, Thomas wheeled his horse forward, and cantered alongside the column. Small spurts of dust kicked from the horse's hooves; the sheer number of people, horses, and mules passing through the moors had already packed and worn the grass to its roots.

Thomas spotted the Earl of York's banners at the front of the army column quickly enough. About half of the other earls were gathered around. Their horses stood nearby, heads bent to graze on the grass yet untrampled by the army.

Thomas swung down from the horse and strode to join them.

For the second time that day, a chill prickled his scalp.

Three men stood in front the Earl of York and the others. They wore only torn and filthy pants. No shoes, no shirt or cloak. Each of the three was gray-white with fear and unable to stand without help.

The chill that shook Thomas, however, did not result from their obvious fear or weakness. Instead, he could not take his eyes from the circular welts centered on the flesh of their chests.

"They've been branded!" Thomas blurted.

"Aye, Thomas. Our scouts found them bound to these trees." The Earl of York nodded in the direction of nearby oaks.

Thomas stared with horror at the three men. The brand marks nearly spanned the width of each chest. The burned flesh stood raised with pus, a long way from the healing that would eventually leave ugly white scars.

Thomas sucked in a breath.

Each brand showed the strange symbol.

"Who...who..."

"Who did this?" the Earl of York finished for Thomas.

Thomas nodded. He fought the urge to glance at the earl's hand to confirm what he didn't want to believe. The symbol that matched the earl's ring. A symbol that had been burned into the grass between two white bulls' heads, adding to the mysteriousness of bulls' hooves arranged in a circle. The symbol of conspiracy.

"It is impossible to tell who did this to these men," the Earl of York answered his own question. "Impossible to understand why they have been left for us to find."

"Impossible?" Thomas could barely concentrate. *"Already the forces of darkness gather…"*

"Yes. Impossible. Their tongues have been removed." The earl shook his head sadly. "Poor men. And of course they cannot write. We shall feed them, rest them, and let them return to their homes."

Could the Earl of York be this fine an actor to stand in front of these tortured men and pretend he had no part of the symbol? Or was his ring simply a bizarre coincidence?

The earl wiped his face clean of sweat.

His ring. Gone.

A tiny band of white marked where the earl had worn it.

Thomas shook off the feeling of being utterly alone.

Surprisingly, Frederick—Frederick the Fat, as Thomas silently called him—proved to be a gracious loser.

"This snot-nose has the teeth of a dragon," he toasted at the council of war that evening.

"Hear, hear," the others responded.

Again, the light of countless campfires spread like flashing diamonds through the valley. Still four days away from the lowland plains and any chance of battle, the army had not dug in behind palisades, and tents were still pitched far enough apart so that neighbors did not have to stumble over neighbors as they searched for firewood or water.

Thomas accepted the compliment with equal graciousness. "As you rightly guessed," he said to Frederick, "the power lies within the bows, not the archers."

"Still," Frederick countered, "the Earl of York has again proven his wisdom. I erred to judge you on age or experience."

Thomas shrugged. Not necessarily from modesty, but rather because the idea for the ingenious modification of the bows had simply been taken straight from his hidden library.

As described within one of his ancient books, running the length of the inside of each bow, Thomas had added a strip of wide, thin bronze, giving more strength than the firmest wood. His biggest difficulty had been finding a drawstring that would not snap under the strain of such a powerful bow.

"But such archery will prove little in this battle." An earl sitting beside Frederick interrupted Thomas in his thoughts. "You have only twenty bows with such a capacity for distance."

Thomas laughed. "Do the Scots know that? They will only understand arrows suddenly reaching them from an unheard-of distance long beyond their own range. Even if they knew our shortage of these bows, each man on the opposing line still realizes it only takes one arrow to pierce his heart. Surely there is benefit in that."

"Yes." Another earl sipped his broth, then continued in support of Thomas. "The man we have dubbed Sir Snot-Nose…"

General laughter. Thomas knew immediately it was a name of affection and honor. He smiled in return.

"Sir Snot-Nose earlier spoke of battle tactics that interest me keenly. I see clearly that even a few of these bows can affect warfare."

The Earl of York strode to the campfire as that statement ended.

All rose in respect.

"You do well, Sir Steven, to make mention of the tactics of war," the Earl of York said grimly in response. "I have just received word from our scouts. It isn't enough to be plagued by the evils of slain white bulls and tongueless men. The Scots' army numbers over four thousand strong."

Silence deepened as each man realized the implications of that news. They numbered barely three thousand. Man against man. Beast against beast. And outnumbered by a thousand. They would be fortunate to survive.

The Earl of York, as was his due, spoke first to break the silence. "Perhaps our warrior, Thomas of Magnus, has a suggestion."

The implied honor nearly staggered Thomas. To receive a request for council among these men...yet still he wondered if the Earl of York was friend or foe. And if a foe, why would he give any honor to Thomas?

"Thank you," Thomas replied, more to gain time and calmness than from gratitude. To throw away this chance...

Thomas thought hard. *These men understand force and force alone. This much I have learned.*

Another thought flashed through his mind, a story of war told him by Sarah, a story from one of the books of ancient knowledge.

He hid a grin in the darkness. Each man at the campfire waited in silence, each pair of eyes studied him.

Finally, Thomas spoke.

"We can defeat the Scots," he said. "First, we must convince them we are cowards."

TWENTY

Katherine's place of encampment was set apart from the others, for many feared the knowledge that an herbalist had about plants and animals. Indeed, any herbalist had to be careful that rumors about witchcraft did not begin.

She was alone, then, when a shadow crossed over her as she crouched to stir the coals of an almost-dead fire with a sharpened branch, green and cut recently from a sapling.

She had known Thomas was approaching, but also knew that an old woman would not have the keen hearing and sharp vision she possessed, so she acted ignorant of his presence, even as he stood above her.

"I have questions for you," he said.

She pretended she could not hear him. Not only was that in character for an old woman, but it gave her time to compose herself for when she would finally rise and look upon his face.

Although she knew that her filthy face and the unruly long and gray hair of the wig gave her the appearance of a hag, with Thomas she wasn't as confident of her disguise as she was when mingling with the peasants and soldiers of the camp.

Thomas was intelligent, an observer, and a man of questions. That made it dangerous enough to be near him. She was also forced to admit to herself that she could not fight her own emotional reaction to him, but could only hope to conceal it.

"I said," Thomas repeated, but louder, "I have questions for you."

"Eh?" Katherine made an awkward turn of her head, careful to keep the gray hair across her face.

"M'lord!" she croaked. She pretended to almost fall as she rose, making it look as though her joints ached and all movement was painful.

She began to bow in respect.

"Please," he said, "find a place to sit."

She moved to a fallen tree and eased herself onto a place between branches that had been removed to feed fires.

"M'lord," she repeated. She fought the temptation to look directly into his face, knowing that it would only lead to thoughts of what it might be like to caress it with her fingers. The night before, when she had been sent as a messenger to get him from the tent for the old man, she had wanted to hold him close and feel his strong arms around her shoulders.

"Something about the way you move," he said, "the cadence of your voice…"

Had he guessed so soon who she was beneath this disguise?

"I am the herbalist you ordered to join your army on this march," she said in the quietest voice possible. "If you have a request of me, I will do my best to oblige. But please don't confuse me with riddles."

He stared for a few moments, then shook his head, more at himself than at her.

"I'm told that, of anyone," he said, "you might have answers for me about the sacrifice of the white bulls."

Katherine squeaked with pretended fright, as any peasant would when confronted with an evil superstition.

"None, m'lord. None!"

She made a movement to push away from him and rise again, but he placed a hand on her shoulders. It would be terrifying if he saw through her disguise. And yet she hoped he would.

"Please," he said. "I have no place to turn but to you. And your fright convinces me that you know more than you want to reveal."

There was a possibility—all too good—that Thomas had long since seen through her disguise. Perhaps he'd known even when he approached her and Hawkwood in the market to inquire about henbane and mandrake and poppy.

Yes, if Thomas had already become one of the Druids, it would serve them to have Thomas pretend ignorance. Then, if Katherine and Hawkwood accepted him into their ranks, he could spy for the Druids.

If so, she could play his game. Cautiously. She would act as if Thomas truly was searching for answers, but make no commitment to expose who she was. The stakes were too great to place trust in Thomas.

"If I speak, I will die," Katherine said, hugging herself and shivering. "The very trees have ears, and they will know what I have revealed and punish me for it."

"Trees do not have ears," he said. "This conversation is only between you and me. And already you have revealed that there is danger, and that someone is part of it. When you say 'they,' who do you mean?"

"No! You trick me with words!"

"I only listen closely."

"I have nothing more to say." To be true to her role, this reluctance was required.

He smiled sadly. "Then I go forth, telling everyone in earshot about the old woman herbalist who revealed all the secrets about the strange symbol. That will get back to them soon enough, and then, if what you fear is true, you most surely will be dead. So choose. Safely tell me what you know, or remain silent and condemn yourself."

To properly play her role, there was only one answer for Katherine to give.

"Go then," she said. "Tell the world I've spilled all that I know. Go then, and pass a death sentence on an old woman. For I will tell you nothing. Either way, you will not gain answers from me."

"You have until three nights from now to change your mind," Thomas said. "If not, you shall be arrested and thrown into my prison until you speak."

TWENTY-ONE

On his horse, Thomas stayed alongside his army as the mass of soldiers marched forward, creaky and bulky, but now with a sense of urgency. The enemy waited three days ahead.

Repeatedly during the day, the Earl of York wheeled his horse beside Thomas and relayed new battle information or confirmed old. It was a clear sign to the other earls that Thomas was fully part of the council of war. Yet Thomas wondered. Did the Earl of York have other reasons for pretending friendliness?

Thomas also noticed little laughter and singing in the marching column. No one had forgotten the grisly sights of the previous day.

"Druids," the old man had said. *"Beware those barbarians from the isle."*

The ones of the strange symbol and the terrifying acts of brutality!

As Thomas swayed to the gentle walk of his horse, he decided there was a way to find out more about Druids, even if the old man of mystery never appeared again.

First, however, there was the formal council of war as camp was made that evening.

The Earl of York wasted no time once all were gathered. "After tonight, there are only two nights before battle. Each of you have reduced by a third the fires in your camps?" he asked.

In turn, each lesser earl nodded, including Thomas.

"Good, good," the Earl of York said. "Already their spies are in the hills. Observing. Waiting."

"You know this to be true?" Frederick asked with slight surprise.

The Earl of York snorted. "Our own spies have been reporting for days now. Only a fool would expect the enemy not to do the same."

"Their fires," Thomas said, "what word?"

"The valleys they choose for camp are filled as if by daylight."

Silence as each contemplated the odds of death against such an army.

The Earl of York did not permit the mood to lengthen. He continued his questions in the tone that made them sound like orders. "All of you have brave volunteers ready to desert our army?"

Each again nodded.

"Tomorrow, then," the Earl of York said, "is the day. Let half of them melt away into the forest. The rest on the following day."

He paused. "Slumber in peace, gentlemen. Dream only of victory."

While all began to leave, the earl moved forward and discreetly tugged on Thomas's sleeve.

"If this battle plan works, friend, your reward will be countless. If not"—the earl smiled the smile of a fighter who has won and lost many times—"it shall be man against man, beast against beast. What say you to that?"

"Then I shall fight bravely, m'lord."

"No, Thomas. What say you to a reward? Let us prepare ourselves for the best. Ask now. What is your wish?"

Thomas thought of the ring. The symbol. And Druids.

Was the Earl of York part of the conspiracy to reconquer Magnus?

If so, would he still honor a promise made?

"Reward?" Thomas repeated quietly. "I would wish simply that you spoke truth to a simple question."

The earl's jaw dropped. He recovered quickly. "You have my word of honor." Then he dryly added, "My friend, in fairy tales, most men ask for the daughter's hand."

Thomas snorted at the unexpected reply. During that moment, he felt at ease with the older man. "I would fear, m'lord, that the daughter might resemble too closely her father."

The earl slapped his belly and roared laughter. "Thomas!" he cried. "You are a man among men. I see a destiny for the likes of you."

Surely, Thomas told himself, this man could not be one of them.

TWENTY-TWO

Thomas cooked his own chicken over a fire to ensure his food would not be poisoned. He'd shared a portion of it with his guards, and taken the remainder with him as he walked to another vantage point.

The sun warmed his shoulders, and Thomas lifted the roasted chicken to his mouth. A rustle of leaves drew Thomas's attention and he half-turned at the sound, just in time to see a cudgel swinging at his head.

He ducked, and the cudgel swooshed over him and cracked into the trunk of a nearby tree.

But there were two attackers, and as Thomas reached for the hilt of his sword, the second was more accurate, and a jarring blow from the other cudgel numbed his arm.

The first man dove at Thomas. He spun sideways to avoid the tackle, but that put him solidly up against a tree with no room to maneuver.

The second man swung again, and Thomas was only able to move his head slightly before the end of the cudgel banged his skull. It knocked him to his knees in a daze.

A third blow, across his ribs, sent him sprawling on the ground.

"Finish him off quickly," one of the voices grunted, "before we're discovered."

"Gold," Thomas croaked. "Take my gold."

"Gold?" the second voice said.

"We've no time!" the first voice said. "He's supposed to be dead."

"How much time does it take to pluck his gold?"

"Here," Thomas said, rolling slightly and reaching beneath him for a pouch. "I'll give you all I have. Just spare me."

"Hah!" the second voice said. "A coward after all."

Thomas found his vision returning. Above him, the two men were grinning in triumph. There was nothing remarkable about their clothing, nothing to give an indication who they were or who had sent them. Just two men, easily in their twenties, with dark hair and bearded faces. Neither carried a sword. In a way, this was not surprising. Swords would have marked them as military men and forced them to wear colors that would identify which earl they served. Otherwise, they would have faced questions walking anywhere through the camp.

"Take his gold then," the first growled. "Let's get this done."

Thomas pulled the pouch into his palm and untied the leather loop that kept it shut.

As the second man reached down, Thomas flung the pouch upward, and white dust sprayed from it.

Quicklime, used to strengthen mortar.

In losing his sword fight to Robert, Thomas had realized that while dust could be a weapon, quicklime was much better.

As the powder made contact with the eyes of the man above him, the moisture of his eyes turned the quicklime into a burning type of acid.

The man screamed, clawing at his face.

Thomas took advantage of the confusion to roll over twice, finding the hilt of his sword as he rose.

He managed to parry the downswing of the cudgel with his sword as the first attacker moved in.

In losing his sword fight to Robert, Thomas had also learned that there were times to push aside any impulse of mercy—that only ruthlessness would allow him to survive.

Without hesitation, Thomas punched as hard as he could, catching the man squarely in the nose.

The man howled, stepping backward.

Both of them clutched their faces.

"Kneel immediately," Thomas gasped through his own pain, "or I'll run you through with this steel."

He needed them captured, and he needed to know who sent them.

Without a word, both dropped to their knees.

That's when a blow from behind caught Thomas across the skull.

Thomas toppled forward, unconscious before hitting the ground.

TWENTY-THREE

When Thomas became aware of the world again, he discovered he was blind. His hands were bound in front of him. His head throbbed.

He was sitting upright, his back against what felt like a tree.

"You are awake," a voice whispered from nearby.

He felt a caress against his cheek.

"You," he said. "From the old man!"

"Yes," she answered.

He felt coolness against his forehead. It felt like she was wiping his face with a wet cloth.

"Drink this," she said. "It will lessen the pain."

She held a cup to his lips and tilted it. He kept his own lips shut, and the liquid spilled down his chin.

"I'm not trying to poison you," she said. "If I wanted you dead, I had plenty of time and opportunity as I bound your hands and blindfolded you."

"If you had good intentions," he retorted, "I would not be bound and blindfolded."

"I had to do it to protect myself," she answered. "You were in need of help, but I can't risk my own capture."

He said nothing to that. She had guessed accurately that if he could, he would not let her escape until she gave him more answers.

"Now drink. You can trust me."

"I doubt that," he grumbled. But this time, when she held the cup to his lips, he opened his mouth and drank. The liquid was bitter and he choked it down.

"It will take a few minutes," she said. "I have placed a knife on the ground. To your left, a few paces away. If you crawl and feel around carefully, you'll be able to find it. Then you can cut yourself loose and remove your blindfold."

That would give her time to escape, he realized.

"Don't go. Tell me what happened!"

"I was following you, and from a distance, I saw the attack of the first two. A third man snuck up behind you. He forced the other two away from you at swordpoint."

"That makes no sense," Thomas said. He groaned. "No sense at all. Who were the men?"

"The third," she said, "wore the colors of the Earl of York."

Someone sent by the earl had attacked him? Yet another reason not to trust a man he liked and wanted to trust.

Or perhaps his attacker from behind was merely wearing the colors of the earl as an act of treachery against the earl. Each answer that Thomas learned, it seemed, only led to more doubts and confusion.

His head began to throb less. Indeed, something in the potion had immediately begun to soothe him. That was no comfort. He was beginning to realize that a knowledge of herbs and roots beyond what the ordinary peasant understood was a marking of those who, it seemed, treated him like a pawn in a cryptic chess game.

"And why were you following me?" he asked.

"Much is at stake. If you want this conversation to continue, tell me what is in your possession that has such value that you must be watched and protected."

He felt anger, but told himself that it was a natural result of his confusion, and that giving in to his emotions would not gain him anything but empty satisfaction.

"Magnus," he said. "My own family lost it to the Mewburns. And I was able to reconquer it. The Mewburns want to regain it, and the power and wealth that comes with it. For all I know, others want to gain Magnus, and you belong to them."

"You are not stupid," she said. "And don't treat me as if *I* am stupid enough to believe that you believe this. If all that was at stake was a mere kingdom, your immediate death would ensure those who want it are free to battle over it. If you want answers before I leave, tell me what you possess of near infinite value."

Thomas wondered what he should reveal. He desperately wanted answers, but to even hint at the books in his possession was to put them in danger. Unless she—and others—already knew about them.

"Knowledge," Thomas finally said with graveness. "To own knowledge that others don't have is to own power. Scientific knowledge can look like magic. Other knowledge, such as that of potions of herbs and roots, gives power over life or death."

"You need not be so coy, Thomas. Say it plainly. Books that contain knowledge beyond anything that is already known in England are priceless. And you have those books."

"If that is so, it would appear that I am caught between two forces battling for those books. Speak plainly in return. Druids are on one side. And the other?"

"Here I cannot yet speak so plainly. Yet. However, this is a battle that has raged for centuries."

Centuries! He wanted to ask more, but sensed from her tone she would not reveal more. Instead, he focused on a different aspect to this puzzle.

"You acknowledge I am caught between two forces? And that the Druids do exist?"

"Unseen to society, manipulating the course of history. Yes."

"And the other side, then, opposes the Druids? You are on the other side?"

"Thomas," she answered, "before I leave, I need to tell you that you are mistaken about the books of knowledge. We both agree that the books you possess are beyond price, literally worth kingdoms. But there is something of greater value that you possess, and until you understand that answer, you cannot become one of us."

"Then at least answer who you are," he said.

"I cannot."

"Then let me say this. All I want for myself is to remain lord of Magnus. I have no interest in choosing sides in some battle that you pretend is so important."

"You need to see beyond Magnus, Thomas. Or you will lose what is of the greatest value of all."

"I need no help and will remain lord of Magnus by my own wits and willpower."

She didn't reply.

"Hello?" Thomas said. "Hello?"

Either she was gone or still watching him. There was only one way to find out.

He sighed and began crawling to his left to find the knife that would free him.

She did not prevent him or speak out. So she had abandoned him. He hoped the knife was there.

It was where she had promised, and he cut the bonds loose by placing the knife between his feet and sawing against it.

He pulled off the blindfold, and although he knew it would be a useless effort, he scanned the trees and the path to look for her.

As promised, she was gone, and, likewise, so was his pain.

TWENTY-FOUR

Late afternoon the next day, Thomas joined the Earl of York at the head of the army column.

From the backs of their horses they overlooked yet another moor valley.

"Thus far, our calculations have served us well," the earl said. "Scouts report the Scottish army is barely a half day away. And beyond here, the moors end at the plains."

Sunlight poured over the western hills. Thomas nodded and shaded his eyes with one hand. He did not trust this man, yet it was important to pretend otherwise.

"This does appear to be the perfect place to ambush an army," Thomas said. "High, sloping hills—impossible to climb under enemy fire. Narrow entrances at both ends—easy to guard against escape. Your scouts excelled in their choice."

Thomas nodded again, and for a moment, both enjoyed the breeze sweeping toward them from the mouth of the valley.

"Well, then. We have made our choice." The Earl of York sighed. "Any army trapped within it is sure to be slaughtered."

He turned and called to the men behind him.

"Send a runner back with directions. We shall camp ahead." He lifted a hand to point. "There. In the center of the valley."

Then quietly, he spoke again to Thomas. "Let us pray the valley does not earn a new name in our honor," the earl said with a shudder. "The Valley of Death."

Thomas shuddered with him. But for a different reason. Even after several days of travel, it still seemed too bright, the pale band of skin on the earl's finger where he had so recently worn a ring.

What game was the earl playing?

⚜

A deep drumroll of thousands of hooves shook the earth, and dawn broke pale blue with the thunder of impending war.

The screams of trumpets ordered the direction of the men and beasts that poured into both ends of the valley. High banners proudly led column after column after column of foot soldiers four abreast, every eye intent on the helpless encampment of tents and dying fires in the center of the valley.

It immediately became obvious that much thought had gone into the lightning-quick attack. Amid shouting and clamor, men and horses moved into rows that were hundreds wide.

Like a giant pincer, the great Scottish army closed in on the camp.

When it finished—barely twenty minutes later—the pincer consisted of a deep front row of pikemen. Behind them, hundreds of archers. Behind the archers, knights on horses.

At first light with stunning swiftness, it was a surprise attack, well designed to catch the enemy at its most vulnerable—heavy with sleep.

Finally, a great banner rose upward on a long pole. Every man in the Scottish army became silent.

It made for an eeriness that sent shivers along the backs of even the most experienced warriors. An entire valley filled with men intent on death, yet in the still air of early morning, the only sound was the occasional stamping of an impatient horse.

Then a strong voice broke that silence. "Surrender in the name of Robert the Bruce, king of the Scots!"

The tents of the Earl of York's trapped army hung limp under the weight of dew. Not one flap stirred in response. Smoke wafted from fires almost dead. A dog scurried from one garbage pit to another.

"We seek to deal with honor!" the strong voice continued. "Discuss surrender or die in the tents that hide you!"

Moments passed. Many of the warriors found themselves holding their breaths. Fighting might be noble and glorious, but to win without risking death was infinitely better.

"The third blast of the trumpet will signal our charge. Unless you surrender before then, all hell will be loosed upon you!"

The trumpet blew once.

Then twice.

And at the edge of the camp, a tent flap opened and a figure stepped outside and began striding toward the huge army. From a hundred yards away, the figure appeared to be a slender man, unencumbered with armor or weapons. It was Thomas, who walked without apparent fear to the voice that had summoned him.

TWENTY-FIVE

The geese in front of Isabelle responded to her clucks and whistles
and to the long stick that she used to nudge stragglers back into
the procession. It was part of her daily duty to herd the geese to whatever water was available. Today she had spied a pond in a small valley
just behind the army's main camp.

Walking toward her was an old cobbler, his trade obvious by the
shoes strung over his shoulder. Respectfully, he stepped aside, his face
hidden in the shadows of his cowl.

He startled her, however, by turning around, moving to her side,
and following her toward the pond.

"I'm not interested in shoes," Isabelle said. "We all wait for the outcome of the battle."

"Neither am I interested in shoes," the old man answered. "But for
the sake of anyone watching, how about we both pretend otherwise?"

She recognized his voice. "Master!"

"You are forgiven for uttering that word in public," he said mildly.
"You are intelligent, and it is obvious that none can overhear our conversation. But don't make the same mistake again."

His voice was calm, but the power and certainty in it gave her a
chill.

"No," she said quietly.

"Good, then." He held out a woman's boot. "Suitable?"

"I could not know unless I gave it close inspection. And were I to do that, I risk losing a goose or two. So for the benefit of anyone watching, I will ignore you."

"Yes," he said. "Intelligent. I'll follow, then, until your geese are in the pond."

It wasn't far, but far enough that Isabelle had time to wonder and fear at his presence here. She'd never seen his face fully, and even now knew he'd taken steps to alter his appearance. A wig, perhaps. Wadded grass in his mouth between teeth and cheeks to make his face fatter.

The geese honked happily as they scattered into the water. Later, when she was ready to move them again, she would lure the leaders out onto land with grain.

Satisfied that all were accounted for, Isabelle turned to the old cobbler and asked for a boot. As she examined it, he spoke.

"I commend you for your initiative," he said. "Word has reached me that assassins attacked Thomas. While they did not succeed in killing him, I understand your motive. You and I have not been in communication. You must have decided that if the cook could not poison him, you would address this danger to our cause another way. I trust you were cautious in hiring the assassins and that no one can link you to them?"

"Mas—" Isabelle cut that word off before she could finish.

"You learn quickly," he said in a soothing voice.

"Cobbler," she began again, her heart pounding at the near error. Had she spoken the word *master* so soon after the earlier admonishment, punishment would have been certain. "I wish I could accept your compliment, but this is the first I have heard of the attack. You say that Thomas survived?"

It was frightening to her, how the Master seemed to know of everything through his network of spies.

"Your concern for him seems genuine," the old cobbler said. "But perhaps it would serve us better if he died. What do you say about this?"

"If you were to arrange his death," she said, "I'm sure it could be used to our advantage. The peasants already are frightened at the other signs of our power. But..."

"But?" Now the old cobbler's voice was silky.

"I had understood you wanted Thomas to join us and that I was to help persuade him. I had understood that he alone held the key to ensuring the destruction of the other side. Why would we want him dead? If he survives the battle against the Scots and we can convince him to join us, he is of far greater value alive."

She felt a desperation that she hoped did not show. Thoughts of Thomas filled her with warm longing that had nothing to do with the hidden battle for Magnus. She felt as though she were fighting to save his life, but could not reveal the real reason she wanted him alive.

The old cobbler studied her. His eyes were like black glass, revealing nothing of his thoughts.

"It was not you, then," he said softly.

"I...I don't understand."

"In arguing to spare Thomas, you have spared your own life."

He took the leather boot from her hand. He reached into his cloak and came out with a vial with a glass stopper. He opened the vial carefully and tilted it until a few drops fell on the toe of the boot.

The leather began to smoke, and within seconds, a hole appeared as a perfect circle. He capped the vial and twisted to ensure the seal was in place.

"My guess was that one of the earls sent men to kill Thomas because they feared his growing influence with the Earl of York. But I could not be certain. When I commended you for initiative, it was only to test whether perhaps the assassins had come from you. And if so, this acid would have been the fate of your father. And you would have learned your lesson."

He paused. "Or perhaps you have already learned it? Never—and that means without exception—take action unless you have been commanded to do so." The horror of the image was bad enough, but Isabelle realized the ultimate horror was in learning that her father's fate depended on her. In essence, he was a hostage.

Twenty-Six

Thomas could barely comprehend the sight as he walked. Filling the horizon in all directions were men and lances and armor and horses and banners and swords and shields and pikes.

Directly ahead, the men of the opposing council of war. Among them, the man who had demanded surrender with that strong, clear voice.

Thomas tried driving his fear away but could not. Was this his day to die?

He could guess at the sight he presented to the men on horseback watching his approach. He had not worn the cloak bearing the colors of Magnus. Instead, he had dressed as poorly as a stable boy. Better for the enemy to think him a lowly messenger. Especially for what needed to be done.

There were roughly a dozen gathered. They moved their horses ahead of their army, to be recognized as the men of power. Each horse was covered in colored blankets. Each man in light armor. They were not heavily protected fighters; they were leaders.

Thomas forced himself ahead, step by step.

The spokesman identified himself immediately. He had a bristling red beard and eyes of fire to match. He stared at Thomas with the fierceness of a hawk, and his rising anger became obvious.

"The Earl of York hides in his tent like a woman and sends to us a boy?"

"I am Thomas. Of Magnus. I bring a message from the Earl of York."

The quiet politeness seemed to check the Scot's rage. He blinked once, then said, "I am Kenneth of Carlisle."

Thomas was close enough now that he had to crane his head upward to speak to the one with the red beard.

Sunlight glinted from heavy battle-axes.

"Kenneth of Carlisle," Thomas said with the same dignity, "the Earl of York is not among the tents."

This time, the bearded earl spoke almost with sadness. "I am sorry to hear he is a coward."

"He is not, m'lord. May we speak in private?"

"There is nothing to discuss," Kenneth said. "Accept our terms of surrender. Or the entire camp is doomed."

"Sir," Thomas persisted, hands wide and palms upward, "as you can see, I bear no arms. I can do you no harm."

Hesitation. Then a glint of curiosity from those fierce eyes.

"Hold all the men," Kenneth of Carlisle commanded, then dismounted from his horse. Despite the covering of light armor, he swung down with grace.

Thomas stepped back several paces to allow them privacy.

Kenneth of Carlisle advanced and towered above Thomas. "What is it you can possibly plead that needs such quiet discussion?"

"I mean no disrespect, m'lord," Thomas said in low tones, "but the surrender which needs discussing is yours."

Five heartbeats of silence.

The huge man slowly lifted his right hand as if to strike Thomas, then lowered it.

"I understand." Yellow teeth gleamed from his beard as he snorted disdain. "You attempt to slay me with laughter."

"No," Thomas answered. "Too many lives are at stake."

Suddenly Kenneth of Carlisle clapped his hands down on Thomas's shoulders and shook him fiercely. "Then play no games!" he shouted.

That surge of temper ended as quickly as it had arrived, and the shaking stopped.

Thomas took a breath. "This is no game." He looked past Kenneth of Carlisle at the others nearby on their horses. They stared back with puzzled frowns.

"I am here to present you with a decision," Thomas continued again to the bearded man. "One you must consider before returning to your horse."

"I shall humor you." Kenneth of Carlisle folded his arms and waited.

"Firstly," Thomas said, "did you believe our army was at full strength?"

After a moment of consideration, the Scottish earl replied, "Certainly not. Our scouts brought daily reports of cowards fleeing your army. The deserters we captured all told us the same thing. Your entire army feared battle against us. We saw proof nightly. Your—"

"Campfires," Thomas interrupted. "Each night you saw fewer and fewer campfires. Obvious evidence of an army that shrunk each day, until last night when you may have calculated we had less than a thousand men remaining."

Kenneth of Carlisle laughed. "So few men we wondered if it would be worth our while to make this short detour for battle."

"It was the Earl of York's wish," Thomas said. He risked a quick look at the tops of the hills, then hid a smile of satisfaction.

"Eh? The Earl of York's wish?"

"Again, with much due respect, m'lord." Thomas swept his arm wide to indicate the valley. "Did it not seem too easy? A crippled army quietly camped in a valley with no means of escape?"

Momentary doubt crossed the man's face.

Thomas pressed on. "The deserters you caught had left our army by the Earl of York's command. Each man had instructions to report great fear among the men left behind. We reduced the campfires to give the impression of mass desertion. While our fires are few, our men remain many."

The news startled Kenneth of Carlisle enough for him to flinch.

"Furthermore," Thomas said, "none of those men are here in the valley. Each tent is empty. In the dark of night, all crept away."

Five more heartbeats of silence.

"Impossible," blurted Kenneth of Carlisle. But the white that replaced the red of flushed skin above his beard showed that the man suddenly considered it very possible, and did not like the implications.

Thomas kept his voice calm. "By now"—Thomas resisted the urge to look and reconfirm what he already knew—"those men have reached their new positions. They block the exits at both ends of this valley and line the tops of the surrounding hills."

"Impossible." This time, his tone of voice was weaker.

"Impossible, m'lord? Survey the hills."

This was the most important moment of the battle. Would the huge man be stunned at their desperate bluff?

What he and Thomas saw from the valley floor seemed awesome. Stretched across the entire line of the tops of the hills, on each side of the valley, men were stepping into sight in full battle gear. From the viewpoint below, those men were simply dark figures, made small by distance. But the line was solid in both directions and advancing downward slowly.

The Earl of York had timed it perfectly.

"Impossible," Kenneth of Carlisle said for the third time. There was, however, no doubt in his voice. Murmuring rose from around them as others noticed the movement. Soon word had spread throughout the entire army. Men started shifting nervously.

"The Earl of York's army will not advance farther," Thomas promised. "Not unless they have reason."

Thomas also knew if the Earl of York's army moved any closer, the thinness of the advancing line would soon become obvious. The row was only two warriors deep—as many as possible had been sent away from the line to block the escapes at both ends of the valley.

"We shall give them reason," Kenneth of Carlisle swore intensely as he drew his sword. "Many will die today!"

"And many more of yours, m'lord."

Kenneth of Carlisle glared and with both hands buried half the blade of the sword into the ground in front of Thomas.

Thomas waited until the sword stopped quivering. "M'lord," he said, hoping the fear would not be heard in his voice, "I requested a discussion in privacy so you and I could reconsider any such words spoken harshly in the heat of anger."

Kenneth of Carlisle glared harder but made no further moves.

"Consider this," Thomas said. "The entrances to the valley are so narrow that to reach one of our men, twenty of yours must fall. Neither is it possible for your men to fight upward against the slope of these hills. Again, you would lose twenty to the Earl of York's one."

"Warfare here in the center of the valley will be more even," Kenneth of Carlisle stated flatly. "That will decide the battle."

Thomas shook his head. "The Earl of York has no intention of bringing the battle to you."

Thomas remembered a quote from one of his ancient books, the one that had given him the idea for this battle plan: *"The skilled commander takes up a position from which he cannot be defeated…thus a victorious army wins its victories before seeking battle; an army destined for defeat fights in the hope of winning."*

"The Earl of York is a coward!" Kenneth of Carlisle blustered.

"A coward to wish victory without killing his men or yours? All your supplies are behind at your main camp. His men, however, will be well fed as they wait. In two or three days, any battle of our rested men against your hunger-weakened men will end in your slaughter."

Kenneth of Carlisle lost any semblance of controlled conversation. He roared indistinguishable sounds of rage. And when he ran out of breath, he panted a declaration of war. "We fight to the bitter end! Now!"

He turned to wave his commanders forward.

"Wait!" The cry from Thomas stopped Kenneth of Carlisle in midstride. "One final plea!"

The Scottish earl turned back, his fiery eyes flashing hatred. "A plea for your life?"

Thomas realized again how close he was to death. And again, he fought to keep his voice steady.

"No, m'lord. A plea to prevent the needless slaughter of many men." Thomas held out his hands. "If you will permit me to hold a shield."

The request was so unexpected that curiosity once more replaced fierceness. Kenneth of Carlisle called for a shield from one of his men.

Thomas grasped the bottom edge and held it above his head so that the top of the shield was several feet higher than his hands.

Let them see the signal, Thomas prayed. *For if battle is declared, the Scots will too soon discover how badly we are outnumbered.*

Moments later, a half-dozen men broke from the line on the hills.

"Behind you, m'lord." Thomas hoped the relief he felt was not obvious. "See the archers approach."

Kenneth of Carlisle half-turned and watched in silence.

The archers stopped three hundred yards away, too far for any features to be distinguished.

"So?" Kenneth of Carlisle said. "They hold back. More cowardice."

"No, m'lord," Thomas said, still holding the shield high. "They need come no closer."

The Scottish earl snorted. "My eyes are still sharp. Those men are still a sixth of a mile away."

Both watched as all six archers fitted arrows to their bows.

"Fools," Kenneth of Carlisle continued in the same derisive tone. "Fools to waste their efforts as such."

Thomas said nothing. He wanted to close his eyes but did not. If but one arrow strayed…

The archers brought their bows up, drew back the arrows, and let loose, all in one motion. A flash of shafts headed directly at them, then faded into nothing as the arrows became invisible against the backdrop of green hills.

Whoosh. Whoosh.

The sound arrived with the arrows, and suddenly Thomas was knocked flat on his back.

For a moment, he thought he'd been struck. Yet there was no piercing pain, no blood. And he realized he'd been gripping the shield so hard from fear that the force of the arrows had bowled him over as they struck the target above his head.

Thomas quickly moved to his feet and looked down to follow the horrified stare of Kenneth of Carlisle. Behind him on the ground lay the leather shield, penetrated completely by six arrows.

Thomas took full advantage of the awe he felt around him. "That, m'lord, is the final reason for surrender. New weaponry. From the hills, our archers will shoot at leisure, secure that your archers will never find the range to answer."

A final five heartbeats of suspense.

Then the huge Scottish earl slumped. "Your terms of surrender?" he asked with resignation.

"The Earl of York simply requests you surrender your weapons. Some of your earls and dukes will be held captive for ransom, of course, but as tradition dictates, they will be well treated. The foot soldiers—farmers, villagers, and peasants—will be allowed to return immediately to their families."

Kenneth of Carlisle bowed his head. "So it shall be," he said. "So it shall be."

Twenty-Seven

L ook here!" It was the camp butcher, sitting near the campfire, enjoying a mug of mead in loud, boisterous company. All were celebrating the bloodless victory and the promise to return to their homes. Shadows played across his broad chest, and when he lifted his mug in a mock toast, dried blood on his fingernails made it look like they were blackened with old bruises. "It's the witch! Back from branding bulls and men!"

His salutation was met with laughter and jeers.

Katherine was in her disguise as the old woman herbalist, and she'd just stepped forward to take a piece of meat, as was due her, from the army provisions.

In response to the joking accusation, Katherine merely lifted her head and stared at the butcher. It was enough to make him squirm, as if she really were considered a witch.

"It was a joke," he muttered. "Really."

"Look at Alfred," a man said with glee from across the fire. "Afraid of an old woman!"

Katherine turned her gaze on this man, who also decided that silence was the best response.

This was the weight of the reputation of an herbalist. The knowledge owned by the herbalist was almost mystical—and like all that was unknown, must be feared.

Katherine stepped away from the fire with the piece of meat dripping fat down her fingers.

She'd approached the fire holding her own mug of mead. Now she drank from it as she moved to the back of the crowd.

The taste was more bitter than she expected, but she forced herself to swallow the liquid anyway.

She took a bite from the meat.

It needed salt. But who among these could afford extra salt? As she chewed, she began to feel lightheaded.

She placed a hand on the shoulder of the man nearest to her to help steady herself.

"Old woman, leave me be," he snarled.

Katherine tried to speak, but her tongue felt like wood. She swayed and fell forward, dimly aware of the man catching her and setting her on the ground.

The stars in the sky turned quickly above her in dizzying circles, and for a moment, she thought she was going to vomit. The urge passed quickly, however, even though the stars kept spinning, to form a circle of blurred light.

The circle grew smaller and smaller, and she realized she was losing her vision.

And her consciousness.

Then all her thoughts ended.

Thomas walked through his camp as his men finished breakfast. Soon, the army would begin to dismantle, and all would journey home.

He sought the old herbalist.

Thomas strode around the fires once, then twice. No one called out to him; his colors clearly marked him as a lord, and avoiding the eye of those in power usually resulted in less work.

Finally, he was forced to attract the attention of a man carrying buckets of water hanging from each end of a pole balanced across his shoulders.

"Tell me, please," Thomas said. "Where is the old herbalist?"

"Last night she fell during the celebrations." The man grimaced. "Too much wine, I would guess. God rest her soul."

Thomas squinted to read the man's face. "God rest her soul?"

"There was nothing that could be done." The man crossed himself quickly. "The butcher was making a few jokes and she fell over and stopped breathing."

"That cannot be!"

The man shrugged, a motion that shook both buckets of water. "She was old, very old. It came as no surprise."

Thomas clamped his mouth shut, then nodded thanks to the man.

What had the crone said? *"Druids. That is a name to be spoken only with great care."*

Surely the herbalist's death was coincidence. Too much wine and too much age and the rigors of daily march. Of course.

Still, Thomas glanced around him often as he joined his men and prepared to return to Magnus.

Somehow, he didn't feel like a victor.

W ould that I had a daughter to offer," the Earl of York said under a wide expanse of sky broken by scattered clouds. "She and a great portion of my lands would be yours."

Thomas flushed.

"Ah, well," the Earl of York sighed. "If I cannot make you my son, at least I can content myself with your friendship."

Thomas wanted badly to be able to trust the man in front of him. Yet there were too many unanswered questions.

Does this man belong to those of the symbol?

Will he betray me? Or I, him?

"Yes, yes," the Earl of York said, letting satisfaction fill his slow words. "The legend of the young warrior of Magnus grows. Even during the short length of our journey back from the Valley of Surrender, tales of your wisdom have been passed repeatedly from campfire to campfire."

Thomas said nothing. He could not, of course, reveal that the strategy had been taken from the secret knowledge that was his source of power. Other worries distracted him as well.

Magnus lies over the next hill, he thought. *Will the Earl of York now honor the reward promised with victory?*

They rode slowly. Thomas returning home with his small army in an orderly line behind. The earl to retrieve his son left at Magnus as a guarantee of safety for Thomas.

Worry washed over Thomas. Who were these Druids of the symbol? What games did the old man play—he who, like the Druids, knew astronomy? From where did he gain such intimate knowledge of Thomas's life? And the castle ahead—would it provide safety against the forces of darkness that had left such terrifying sights for all to see on the march northward?

"Your face grows heavy with dread," the Earl of York joked. "Is it because of the question that burns so plainly in your restlessness over the last few days? Rest easy, my friend. I have not forgotten your strange victory request."

He calls me friend. *Surely this man cannot be a part of the darkness...* Thomas steeled himself.

From the marchers behind him, voices grew higher with excitement and anticipation. This close to home, the trail winding through the moors was very familiar to the knights and foot soldiers. Within an hour they would crest the hill above the lake that held the island castle of Magnus.

There can be no good time to ask, Thomas told himself. He forced his words into the afternoon breeze.

"Your ring, m'lord. The one that carries the evil symbol burned upon the chests of innocent men, the one you removed before the battle. I wish to know the truth behind it."

The earl abruptly reined his horse to a halt and stared Thomas full in the face.

"Any question but that. I beg of you."

Thomas felt his heart collapse in a chill of fear and sadness. "I must, m'lord," he barely managed to whisper. "It carries a darkness that threatens me. I must know if you are friend or foe."

"Friend," the earl answered with intensity. "I swear that upon my mother's grave. Can such a vow not suffice?"

Thomas slowly shook his head.

The earl suddenly slapped his black stallion into a trot. Within seconds, Thomas rode alone.

THIRTY

Two others also traveled back to Magnus, but with much less fan-fare than the triumphant army returning home. These two avoided the main path through the moors and walked slowly, with caution.

Even during the warmth of daylight, the first figure remained well wrapped in black cloth. A casual observer would have aptly blamed it upon the old age so apparent by his cane and stooped shoulders, since old age often left bones aching with chill.

The second figure, however, walked tall and confident with youth. When the wind rose, it swept her long hair almost straight back.

They moved without pause for hours, so steadily that the casual observer would have been forced to marvel at the old man's stamina—or urgency. They finally rested at a secluded spot in the hills directly above the lake and castle of Magnus.

"I have no desire to risk you there," Hawkwood said, pointing his cane downward at the village in the center of the lake. "But Thomas will learn the earl's son has disappeared from the castle."

"That makes no sense."

"It could only be Druids. The castle's secret passages are known to them as much as to us."

"It's not the escape that surprises me," she said. "But that they might choose to tip their hand. Isn't Thomas first going to wonder why? The war is over. There is no need for escape. And then isn't Thomas going to wonder how it was possible?"

"Those were my first thoughts too. I fear this is a bold move that marks the beginning of the Druid attempt to reconquer Magnus."

"There is little risk for me," the young woman said. "My disguise served me well during my time in Magnus and will continue to do so."

The old man arched an eyebrow barely seen in the shadows that surrounded his face. "Katherine, you were a child during most of your previous time in Magnus, not a near-woman, now in love."

She blushed. "Is it that apparent?"

Hawkwood shook his head. "Only in little ways. The joy on your face as we discussed a method to reach Thomas during his march to the lowland plains of battle. Your sighs during those days after our midnight meeting, when we followed the army to the Valley of Surrender. And your trembling that morning on the hillside as we waited the outcome of his plan against the Scots."

Her blush deepened. "Thomas is worthy. I had much opportunity to watch him in Magnus. And now, perhaps my feelings will give me courage to help him as he needs."

Hawkwood suddenly struck a slab of rock with his cane. "No!"

He looked at the now-broken cane, then looked at her. His voice softened. "Please, no. Emotions are difficult to trust. Until we are certain which side he has chosen, he cannot know of you, or of the rest of us. The stakes are far too great. We risk your presence back in Magnus for the sole reason that—despite all we've done—he is or might become one of them. Love cannot cloud your judgment of the situation."

She ran both her hands through her hair. "You were not there," she whispered, almost to herself, "the day he attacked a man for insulting a poor, hideous freak. You did not see the rage in his eyes that someone so helpless should suffer. Thomas will not sell his soul. He will not be seduced by a promise of Druidic power."

Hawkwood sighed. "Beneath your words, you say something else. That you don't want to be his executioner."

Katherine nodded. "It was bad enough becoming my own executioner. I do not want to kill him too."

THIRTY-ONE

At the entrance to the valley of Magnus, Thomas saw the Earl of York sitting on his horse beneath the shade of a tree well aside of the trail.

The Earl of York waved once, then beckoned.

Thomas slowly trotted his own horse to the tree.

The noise of travel faded behind him, and when Thomas reached the earl, he was greeted with a silence interrupted only by the buzzing of flies and a swish and slap as the other horse swung its tail to chase away the insects.

The blue of the lake surrounding Magnus broke through gaps of the low-hanging branches, and dappled shadows fell across the earl's face. It was impossible to read anything in his eyes.

"We part here," the earl said. "I trust you will send me my son as soon as you are assured that I have not dealt in any treacheries by sending soldiers to Magnus in your absence."

"Come with me now," Thomas said. "Meet him yourself and travel together."

"I've been away from my army too long already today. If you give my son an escort, he and the riders will catch us soon enough." Then the earl sighed. "I should not deceive you in this. My son and I are like strangers to each other. He is not comfortable in my presence, nor am I comfortable in his. I tell myself I need to find a way to mend whatever is broken between us, but now is not the time."

"I am sorry to hear of your estrangement," Thomas said.

The earl shrugged, but it was a move that poorly hid his emotional pain. "I should not have burdened you with that."

"No burden," Thomas answered. "I suggest that I wait until to-morrow to send him with an escort. When I reach Magnus, it will be too close to evening, and I would rather not risk sending him on a journey in the dark."

"Thank you," the earl said. "You will receive an invitation from me soon to join me at a victory feast and a place of honor at my table."

"I look forward to it. Fare well on your journey home."

"Nothing else? No demand to force me to honor my vow in regards to your question?"

"No demand," Thomas said. "There would be no honor in that for me. Or for you."

"Yes," the earl said. "You have the mark of a man who lets other men live their lives as they choose."

Thomas gazed steadily in return. "The man who betrays another also betrays himself. Often that is punishment enough."

The Earl of York shook his head. "From where do you get this wisdom?"

"What little I have was given by a dear teacher, now dead."

More silence.

By then, almost the entire small army, in its rush to reach home, had passed along the trail. Then final puffs of dust fell to rest as the last straggler moved on, and in the quiet left behind, the earl began again.

"I have waited here in deep thought and anguish," he said. "I have two confessions to make to you. For the first I will not ask forgiveness.

It was required for us to triumph against the Scots. I was forced to make a choice between two evils. Thomas, I was the one who struck you unconscious after you defeated the two men sent to kill you."

Thomas held his gaze steady as the earl continued.

"The day they attacked, I was trying to join you to speak to you about tactics. Then I saw them following you, and waited to see what they wanted. When I realized they were going to attack you, I was too far away to help, and by the time I had arrived, you had won the fight and were demanding to know who sent them. I struck you to gain their confidence and learn the answer for myself, then left you there when I was satisfied you were not seriously hurt. Can you think of a reason why I did not want you to hear the answer from them?"

Thomas gave it some thought and nodded. "Because once I knew, I would take action."

"We could not afford to have fighting within our own camp. It was Frederick, who feared you were gaining too much power and influence. He wanted you out of the way."

The earl paused. "He has paid the price, believe me. He will be losing his land and title, and sent to London for punishment. Edward II will not take it lightly that Frederick did not put aside his own interests to stay unified with the rest of us against the Scots. I would suggest you take this no further."

"As you wish," Thomas said. And waited.

"My ring," the earl said. "My second confession is that the ring is a shameful secret, passed from father to son through many generations." He smiled weakly. "Alas, the debt I owe and a promise made justly demands that now the ancient legend be revealed to one outside the family."

Thomas still waited.

"The symbol belongs to a group of high priests with dark power. We know only their name, not the men behind the name," the earl almost whispered.

"Druids," Thomas said.

"How could you know? It's not possible!"

"From the isle of the Celts. Men now hidden among us."

"Thomas, your knowledge is frightening," the Earl of York said quickly. "Most who speak that name soon die."

Thomas smiled grimly. "That promise has already been made. Why else do I drive you to answer me all?"

The Earl of York sighed. "Then I shall tell all."

He climbed down from his horse and motioned for Thomas to do the same, then gazed at the far lake of Magnus as he spoke in a flat voice.

"In our family, the ring is passed from father to eldest son, the future Earl of York. With it, these instructions: acknowledge the power of those behind the symbol or suffer horrible death. And our memory is long. Five generations ago, the Earl of York refused to listen to a messenger—one whose own ring fit into the symbol engraved upon the family ring. Within weeks, worms began to consume his still-living body. No doctor could cure him. Even a witch was summoned. To no avail. They say his deathbed screams echoed throughout the castle for a week. His son—my great-great-grandfather—then became the new Earl of York. When he outgrew his advisers, he took great care in acknowledging the power that had been passed to him."

Thomas felt the chill of the earl's voice. "Acknowledging the power?"

"Yes," came the answer. "A favor asked. A command given. Rarely more than one in an earl's lifetime. Sometimes none. My great-grandfather did not receive a single request. My father…"

The earl's voice changed from flat to sad. "My father obeyed just one command. It happened over twenty years ago. I was old enough to understand his pain. Yet he obeyed."

A thought clicked within Thomas. *Over twenty years ago...*

"Your father stood aside while Magnus fell," Thomas said with sudden insight. "Despite allegiance and protection promised, he let the new conquerors reign."

The Earl of York nodded.

It explained much! Thomas had sworn to Sarah on her deathbed that he would reconquer Magnus to avenge the death of his parents, the former and rightful rulers of Magnus who had been dethroned over twenty years ago.

Then Thomas drew a deep breath as he realized the implications.

It cannot be. But he knew it was.

"Having lost it," Thomas gritted, "these Druids now demand Magnus be returned. The horrifying rituals plain to see along the march—a message for you perhaps." Then came the implication he dreaded.

"Or a message for you," the Earl of York said slowly as he finally turned to face Thomas. His face showed the gray pallor of anguish.

"Thomas, I call you friend. Yet twice along the march, in the dark of night, I was visited by one of the ring."

Thomas did not blink as he held his breath against the words he did not want to hear.

The earl's voice dropped to little more than a croak. "Each time, Thomas, I received warning to expect that payment for my family's power is soon due."

THIRTY-TWO

The chamber was so narrow and tight that Katherine was forced to stand ramrod straight. Even so, the stone of the walls pressed painfully against her knees and elbows.

She had stood that way, fighting cramps of pain, in eight-hour stretches each of the previous two days, with rough stone pressing so tightly she scraped against it with the slightest of movements. In the tight confines of darkness and ancient stone, red, raw skin and rigid muscles were the price she paid to spy on Thomas.

Unlike some of the other hidden passages in the castle, necessity of concealment here required the chamber be small, for there was no other way it could be hidden in a hollowed portion of the thick rear wall of the throne room. Tiny vents in the cracks of stone—at a height barely above Katherine's waist and invisible to anyone inside the room—brought air upward into the space.

The vents did not allow light into the chamber, only sound, carried so perfectly that any word spoken above a whisper reached Katherine's ears.

She had no fear of being detected. As Hawkwood had instructed before sending her back to Magnus, the entrance to the chamber was fifty feet away, hidden in the recesses of a little-used hallway. To slip in or out, she need simply stand in the recess until enough quietness had convinced her that entry or exit was safe.

More difficult than avoiding detection, however, was navigating the twisting blackness of the tunnel that led through the thick castle walls to the chamber behind the throne room. More than once, she had felt the slight crunch from stepping on the fur and bones of long-dead and dust-dry mice and—she shuddered—bats. Her first time through, two days earlier, had been a gagging passage through cobwebs that brushed her face in the darkness with no warning and clung to her like eerie silk.

Remember Hawkwood and his instructions, she told herself as yet another cramp bit into her left thigh. *This is a duty we have performed for generations.*

Two days of petitions and complaints. Two days of the slowly considered words given in return by the lord, Thomas of Magnus. Two days of exquisite torture, listening and loving more the man who might never discover the secret of her hidden face. But not once, the expected Druid messenger.

Yet the Druid would arrive. Hawkwood had so promised, and Hawkwood was never wrong.

Katherine snapped herself away from her thoughts and listened to another verdict, delivered so crystal-clear into the chamber.

"No, Gervaise, there will not be any more money supplied from the treasury for church charity. Unless you supply me an answer to something that keeps me awake every night."

"Another one of your questions about God and His mysterious nature?"

"No. Even more difficult to answer than that. You know that the earl's son escaped."

"Of course."

"How?" Thomas asked. "That is what I need to know. It's as if the very castle itself is a mystery."

"I have no answer."

"And why would the earl's son take such a risk? If caught, it would mean death. Yet he must have heard about our victory. Had he waited but half a day, I would have not only released him but sent him with an armed escort to protect him on his journey."

"I have no answer to that either."

"Then," Thomas said, with what sounded like an attempt at light-heartedness, "I have no choice but to withhold money from the church charity."

"But my lord, you know both questions were impossible for me to answer."

Thomas's sigh reached Katherine with as much clarity as his light-hearted tone had done before. "Gervaise, much as you pretend surprise, you expected that decision from me. You know, as I do, that many are now tempted to forsake work for the ease of charity meals."

Gervaise chuckled. "What do you propose? Every day, one or two more appear at the church doorsteps."

"Get the Father to deliver long sermons. Ones that must be endured as a price to pay for the meals."

Laughter from both.

Then a more sober tone from Thomas. "I jest, of course. Instead, find work on the church building or its grounds," he said. "Any work. Let those who are able contribute long hours, enough so that it is more profitable for them to seek employment elsewhere. You will soon discover who is truly needy."

"Excellent," Gervaise said. "I look forward to our evening walk and discussion. You may tell me more about Katherine."

In the chamber, Katherine's ears began to burn from embarrassment. It was one thing to spy for noble purposes, another to listen to a private conversation. Yet she found herself straining to catch every word.

"Yes. Katherine. If she were another, my world might be perfect…"

Katherine could not help but feel a warm flush of hope at those words. Another…did he mean her? Was he thinking of the time she had been allowed to reveal herself to him in the moonlight? Or did he still dream of Isabelle?

She was given no time to ponder.

"M'lord. One waits here outside," a sentry called into the throne room.

Katherine, of course, could only imagine the silent good-bye salutes between Thomas and Gervaise, and the voice she heard moments later sent an instinctive fear deep inside her.

"Thomas of Magnus." Not a question, but almost a sneer. The voice was modulated and had no coarse accent of an uneducated peasant.

"Most extend courtesy with a bow," Thomas replied, immediately cold.

"I will not prolong this through pretense," the voice replied. "I am here to discuss your future." A pause. Then the voice spoke quickly. "Don't! You draw breath to call for a guard, but if you do, you will never learn the secrets of this symbol, nor of Magnus."

The Druid messenger.

Katherine no longer felt the ache of stiff limbs. Every nerve tingled to listen further.

"I grant you little time," Thomas replied.

"No," came the now soft and triumphant voice. "I have as long as I like. Dread curiosity is plain to read on your face."

"Your time slips away as you speak. What is your message?"

The sneering voice came like a soft caress. "The message is simple, as when you first heard it from Isabelle. Join our circle, remain earl, and gain great power beyond comprehension. Or deny us and lose Magnus."

"Why should I not have you seized and executed?" Thomas asked after a long silence.

"For the same reason that you still live. After all, we have a thousand ways to kill you. An adder, perhaps, slipped into your bedsheets as you sleep. Undetectable poisons. A dagger in your heart. You still live, Thomas, because your death does not serve our purpose. Just as my death now would not serve yours."

"No?" Thomas asked.

"No. You and I, of course, are merely representatives. Your death would only end your life. It would not return to us the power over the people of Magnus, who—before your arrival—were sheep to be handled at our whim."

Short silence. Then from Thomas, "And you represent?" He said it with too much urgency.

The messenger laughed, a cruel sound to Katherine in her hiding spot. "Druids. The true masters of Magnus for centuries."

"Not possible," Thomas said. But Katherine heard enough of a waver in his voice to know he did think it possible.

"Not possible?" the voice countered. "Ponder this. Magnus is an incredible fortress. A king's fortune ten times over could not pay for the construction of this castle and the protective walls. Yet to all appearances, Magnus is located far, far from the bases of power. Why go to the expense, if not for a hidden purpose?"

No! Katherine wanted to scream. *Lies!*

"And," the voice moved like an arched finger slowly scratching a cat's throat, "why has Magnus existed so long without being seriously challenged by the royalty of England? The Earl of York leaves it in peace. So did the Norman kings. And the Anglo-Saxons before them. Would not even a fool decide great power lies within Magnus, great enough to deflect kings for centuries?"

No! Katherine raged inwardly. *Thomas must not believe this!*

"Why did the former lord, Richard Mewburn, take Magnus by the foulest treachery?" Thomas said with hesitation. "If you speak truth, it would seem to me that your circle would control this castle's destiny."

"Of course," came the snorted reply. "That's exactly why Mewburn was allowed to conquer Magnus. He was loyal to us. The earl before him..."

"Yes?" Thomas asked with ice in his voice.

"Don't be a child! We know you were raised at that forsaken monastery, but by someone who told you lies about Magnus."

"She did not!"

"And what evidence do you have to prove it one way or another?"

No reply.

Katherine almost needed to force herself to breathe. She dimly felt her nails biting into her palms but still did not unclench her fists.

Thomas, don't accept their lies! Please, don't force me to be your executioner!

In the heartbeats that followed, Katherine agonized. Thomas did not know enough to make a decision, yet there was no way she and those she served could have risked giving him the truth.

"I have considered the possibility that she lied," Thomas said finally. "And logically, there is no reason against it. I was an orphan and depended upon her for much. It would be difficult for a lost child to recognize the difference between truth and falsehood."

If Katherine could have slumped in that cramped hollow, she would have. Instead, it felt as if her blood drained into a pool at her feet.

I now wish he had never looked into my eyes, she told herself, *and had never raised hopes of love.*

"Good, good," the voice said, now as if it were the cat satisfied with a finger soft against its throat. "We much prefer that you choose to live as one of us. You will share the mysteries of darkness with us, and anything you wish will become yours."

"It must have a price," Thomas said, almost defeated. "The rewards may be plain to see, but loyalty has its demands."

"Thomas, Thomas," the voice chided. "We wish only one thing as a test of your commitment."

"Yes?" Now the pleading of total defeat.

"Your hidden books of knowledge. We must have them."

If he agrees, Katherine told herself, *nothing will ease the pain of my duty. Yet he cannot lead them to the books. I must force my hands to betray my love for him, and tonight he will die.*

"Go," Thomas said with sudden strength and intensity. "Go back to the isle of the Celts!"

Katherine blinked in her darkness.

"Yes!" Thomas raged. "Report back to your murdering barbarian masters that Thomas of Magnus will not bend to those who brand the chests of innocent men."

"Yet—"

"Yet it appeared I might pledge loyalty? Only to see what it was you truly wished. Now, I shall do everything in my power to prevent you from attaining that desire."

"Fool!" The word sounded as if it were molten iron, spat bright red from a furnace. "Magnus shall be taken from you as it was given. By the people."

"That remains to be seen," Thomas said in a steady voice.

THIRTY-THREE

The Earl of York stared in disbelief at his son, Michael, a tall, thin young man with a bloody bandage on his head, who held out a small, circular piece of flesh in the center of his palm.

The two of them were alone in the stables at his castle in York.

The earl had been about to ride his favorite black stallion on an inspection of nearby fields of grain, but news of the return of his son had delayed it. Now the earl stood beside the saddled stallion, his hand on the horse's ribs where he'd been patting it when his son had approached.

Unaware that his hand had frozen against the horse's side, the earl glanced at the piece of flesh in Michael's open hand and then back to the blood-stained bandage that covered the top left side of his son's head.

"Bandits?" the earl said. "They shall be hunted down and hung without trial."

"No," Michael said. "Thomas of Magnus."

"What?" The earl was stunned.

"Furthermore, he told me to show you this and asked me to pass along a message."

"Thomas cut off your ear," the earl said heavily, still unable to absorb what his eyes told him.

"He cut it off himself. And took satisfaction in doing it."

Normally, the smell of hay and straw and horse comforted the earl. He loved to ride and hunt. On horseback, away from the burdens of his power, he felt the most free.

As the earl drew in a deep breath, none of those smells gave him the usual enjoyment. Instead, he fought an outburst of rage.

The earl let out his breath, feeling under control again.

"Thomas also gave me a letter for you," Michael said.

Michael fumbled with a pouch, a difficult move because he was obviously reluctant to simply drop his own ear and throw it away.

"Straight from Thomas of Magnus," Michael said, handing a sealed letter across to the earl. "I watched him write it myself."

The earl examined the wax seal and satisfied himself that it showed the emblem of Magnus. He opened it and read it from where he stood beside the horse.

I have no interest in accepting an invitation for a place of honor at your victory feast. My obligation to you was fulfilled when I led the defeat of the Scots. Further, I will only agree to a pact of allegiance once I receive a payment of gold for my services during the march against the Scots. Ensure that it completely fills the chest I have sent back with your son. If it does not arrive within a fortnight, I will consider your inaction to be a declaration of war. As proof of the seriousness of my intent to wage battle against you if you do not send the gold, look no further than the ear I have taken from your son.

The earl slowly folded the letter. "I still cannot believe Thomas did this."

"I am your son. You think I tell a lie?"

"You have lied to me before. Let's not fool ourselves. It would serve you well for me to war against Magnus, for then it would belong to you someday."

Michael showed scorn. "If I were to lie about this, I would have to keep my head covered the rest of my life around you."

Slowly Michael unwound the bandage.

He turned a side of his head toward the earl, showing a bloody ridge.

The earl gritted his teeth.

"Make note of what I have sworn in this moment," the earl said between those gritted teeth. "We shall keep your ear. After Magnus falls, I'll ensure that Thomas eats it before he faces the hangman."

THIRTY-FOUR

Thomas paced his bedchamber as late-afternoon sun lit the stone floors through the shutters he'd thrown open to the window on the west side.

Eyes closed, Thomas ran his fingers along one of the walls.

The ultimatum delivered by the messenger had served to remind Thomas of what he'd set aside because of the war against the Scots—his need to understand how the ghost of Isabelle had come to him in his bedchamber with a similar message.

He was almost prepared to believe that the event had not occurred, that it had been hallucination. After all, to himself he'd nearly proven without doubt that his food that evening had been laced with a type of poison that would alter his senses. The notation in his books about the symptoms of henbane matched very closely how he'd felt upon waking to the presence of Isabelle—sluggish to the point of immobility, the sensation of being tied in place.

Then, his tamed mouse had gone in those dizzying circles from a taste of stew, dropping as if dead, only to wake slowly a short time later.

His cook, too, had gone blind and insane. Thomas guessed the cook had been poisoned to ensure Thomas could not find out who had instructed him to tamper with the food.

Yet, as convinced as Thomas was that he'd fallen under the spell of a potion on the night of the visit by Isabelle, and as much as he wanted to believe in a simple explanation such as hallucination, he had to choose otherwise.

After all, Isabelle had been essentially a harbinger of the messenger who had just spoken to Thomas. It would be too much of a stretch to believe Thomas's own mind had conjured up an image of Isabelle in anticipation that someday the Druids would send someone else.

No. Since Thomas was highly skeptical of the existence of ghosts, he could only conclude it had been Isabelle. That left him another difficult question—how had she been brought back to life? But he'd decided he would deal with that only if he could answer a secondary question. How had she entered and departed from his bedchamber?

The logical answer was a hidden entrance somewhere. And as daughter of the former lord, Isabelle, it was natural to assume, would have knowledge of any secret passageways in the castle. So now, Thomas was diligently doing what he had had no time to accomplish earlier—a thorough search of the walls.

He closed his eyes, deciding that he would force himself to rely on a sense of touch with his fingers. He was hoping to find a seam or any other indication of a break in the carefully mortared stone.

After an hour inspecting every surface, Thomas changed his tactics.

He had a small hammer, and methodically, he lightly tapped on every stone, listening for hollow points.

That took another hour.

He was unsuccessful with that too.

Thomas felt no sense of frustration or impatience. There must be another way in or another way out. Eventually, he would find it.

He sat on a chest at the foot of his bed to give it more thought.

The sunlight angled to the fireplace on the far wall, and something caught the light as it waved slightly in the breeze that blew through the open shutters.

He stood and walked over to examine it.

It was a single white thread, caught in a rough piece of mortar.

White.

The same color as the dress Isabelle had worn the night she delivered her message.

He began to examine the stones around it more closely.

But he was interrupted by a knock on his door.

"M'lord!" It was Robert's voice.

Thomas didn't like the alarm he heard, and he hurried to open the door.

"What is it?" Thomas asked.

"The Earl of York," Robert said. "I've received word he is marching in our direction. With an army."

THIRTY-FIVE

As he walked through the depths of the castle to the prison cells, Thomas made efforts to breathe through his mouth. Although he insisted that the prisoner get a clean bed of straw every day and that his waste bucket was promptly dumped, it was impossible to avoid the stench that came with imprisonment in tight, dark quarters.

He was in a difficult position. A guard had delivered the message that Geoffrey wanted to see him and had information important to him. On one hand, yes, Thomas was curious and yes, the information might be vital to Thomas. On the other hand, responding to Geoffrey showed a degree of desperation—something Thomas certainly felt—that put Thomas in a weak position.

He stopped in the shadows between two lit torches and realized that showing weakness was not worth whatever information Geoffrey might give him.

He made a decision—one that perhaps he could have made much sooner if his friend Sir William had remained with him at Magnus. Thomas felt he could certainly use the knight's wisdom and guidance.

Thomas turned back and climbed the steps to take him to the throne room. As he passed a guard, he gave simple orders.

"Shackle and blindfold Geoffrey, and escort him to me."

Much better, Thomas told himself. Geoffrey could feel a degree of helplessness as he became a supplicant to Thomas.

"You've heard the tale of the boy who cried wolf," Thomas told Geoffrey.

The man in front of him tilted his head, tracking Thomas by sound, not sight. Geoffrey's skin was gray, his face greasy. His appearance put him among the dregs of criminals, yet his posture reflected a man of royalty.

Thomas felt an instinctive hatred for the man, but continued calmly. "The boy, as you recall, was able to cry wolf twice and the villagers believed both times. It was the third time, when the wolf was really there, that the villagers ignored him. You, however, have only one chance. If you have no information of value to give, no matter how you plead with the guards, you will not get another audience with me."

"Soon," Geoffrey said, "you'll bow to me."

"That was your one chance," Thomas said. "A threat is not information."

To the guards, Thomas gave a curt order. "Take him away."

Geoffrey cackled. "You refuse to bow to the Druids. Here is the prophecy."

"Take him away," Thomas said.

As two guards grabbed him by the elbows, one on each side, Geoffrey let himself go limp so they had to drag him. "Wasn't it enough to see the power of the Druids when Isabelle visited you from the dead? That was the first sign. And the next is this. Before the hour is out, bats will fall from the sky."

This was a disturbing message, especially because Thomas could see its effect on the guards, who looked up involuntarily as if expecting bats to fall from the stone ceiling.

Thomas doubted it would happen, so it wasn't the prophecy that frightened him.

Instead, it was the fact that Geoffrey had spoken about Isabelle's nighttime visit, whether she was a ghost or someone risen from the dead. It wasn't something Thomas had told anyone.

So how had Geoffrey known?

⚜

Tiny John walked the streets of Magnus toward the church when the first howl sounded.

Those around him cocked their heads.

"Listen! What's that?"

"Two dogs fighting, I'd say."

"No, not quite."

"What's going on?"

Then the boy's skin prickled.

Another unearthly howl.

Within moments, the shrieking chorus filled Magnus.

Dogs—in the streets, under carts, in sheds—all through Magnus moaned and howled and barked. People stopped and stared around in amazement. The howling grew louder and more frenzied.

An uneasy feeling filled him, one that had nothing to do with the almost supernatural noise of the dogs. He wanted to hold his head and shake away the grip of something he couldn't explain.

Now cats. The high-pitched scream of yowling cats gradually became plain above the yipping and howling of dogs. All people stood where they were, frozen in awed dread. Rats scurried from dark hiding places, from the corners of market stalls, from the holes among stone walls, and in dozens of places ran headlong and uncaring across the feet of shopkeepers and market people.

Then, unbelievably, *bats*!

Dozens fell from the sky. A great swarm circled frantically a hundred feet above Magnus, each bat dipping and swooping in a crazed dance to exhaustion.

Bats do not fly during the daytime, Tiny John told himself as he struggled to accept what his eyes told him. *They do not drop like a hailstorm of dark stones.*

Still the bats fell. Onto thatched roofs. Onto the carts of shopkeepers. Onto the dried, packed dirt of the streets.

The thud of their landing bodies was lost among the howling and shrieking of cats and dogs. And into the racket came the screams of terrified peasants.

A final dozen bats dropped from the sky to quiver and shake in death throes. The dogs stopped howling. The cats stopped shrieking. And, stunned by the sudden end of the animals' noise, the terrified peasants stopped screaming.

Whispers began.

"A judgment from God," someone said.

"Yes," another said, more clearly. "We allow a murderer of monks to remain lord of Magnus!"

"The Earl of York brings justice with his army!"

"God's judgment!"

"Yes! God's judgment upon us!"

The whispers around them in the marketplace became shouts of anger and fear. Bats lay strewn in all directions.

Tiny John's mouth was dry. He forced himself to swallow. "Thomas must hear of this," he whispered. "If he hasn't been informed already."

THIRTY-SIX

Katherine reached the secluded grove long after the final bells of midnight had rung clearly across the valley from within Magnus. More than once, bent and covered in shawls, she had by necessity played the role of a disoriented servant seeking her tent in the darkness to get by the sentries posted by the Earl of York's army, now camped at the edge of the valley surrounding Magnus. And each time she had faced a sentry, she had gripped her dagger tightly beneath her shawl. Nothing, she told herself, must keep her from Hawkwood.

The long walk along the valley bottom through the black of night had not been simple either. In her mind, each rustle of leaves, each sway of branches, each tiny movement was a falling bat or a scurrying rat. Before, the night had held nothing to frighten her. Now, after the horror of those brief moments in Magnus, it was difficult to imagine she had ever traversed the dark with ease.

Her nerves, however, had not prevented her from making steady progress. Step by step, tree by tree, clearing by clearing, she had moved toward the prearranged meeting place.

As always, Hawkwood was waiting as promised.

He wasted no time with greetings. Nor in seeking identification. Only Katherine would know of this place, or that he would be here each night at this time.

"What happens in Magnus?"

She felt a brief pride that he trusted her enough to assume she succeeded in her mission.

"As you foresaw," Katherine said, "those of darkness sent a messenger."

"And as you predicted," the old man said after some thought, "he refused to be bullied or bribed."

"Yes, but how do you know of—"

"Katherine, had you been forced to be his executioner, nothing could have hidden it in your voice. Thus, I know he is alive. And alive only because he wants no part of the Druids."

"There is more," she said, and explained the morning's happenings and the rumbles of fear within Magnus at the apparent signs of the supernatural.

The old man mused for several minutes. "Your fear is legitimate, my child. Kings—no matter what they wish to believe—rule only by the consent of the people. History is scarred by the revolutions against fools who believed otherwise. Thomas may indeed lose Magnus."

"And Thomas grieves," Katherine told the old man. "He is bewildered by the earl's declaration of war, and moreover by his fierce anger. Thomas once believed they were friends."

Katherine explained the savage message delivered late that afternoon by scroll. Unconditional surrender or unconditional death.

"He is in danger. Not directly because of the siege. But because of the events."

Katherine nodded. "The dogs. The cats. Bats falling dead from the sky. Now that the people within Magnus believe justice must be served against Thomas, he may lose his lordship the same way he gained it."

"I catch doubt of his innocence even in your voice, child."

Katherine sighed. "Slight doubts only. How could our enemies be capable of calling bats to hurl themselves down from the sky?"

"It is a question not easily answered," Hawkwood agreed. "Let me think."

Katherine knew better than to speak again.

He then sat cross-legged and arranged his mantle over him to fend off the cold night air. He seemed to slip into a trance.

Katherine waited. And knew too well how long that wait might be. She waited as the cold seeped into her. She waited as her tired legs grew to feel soreness even more. She waited in silence broken only by distant muttering of owls and the light skipping of mice across leaves.

Not until the gray fingers of false dawn reached into the valley did Hawkwood stir.

When he finally spoke, it was gentle.

"Close your eyes," he said to Katherine. "Do you recall if you saw smoke as the creatures howled in Magnus?"

She did as instructed. Eyes closed lightly, at first she saw only the frantic movement of bats against the morning sky. Then, dimly, something snagged in her memory because it did not belong against that sky.

"Yes," she said with triumph. "Smoke from the bell tower of the church!"

Hawkwood let out held breath. "And you say you felt as if you should shake your head free from a grip you couldn't explain."

Katherine nodded. In the cold dawn, slight wisps rose white from her mouth with the rise and fall of her chest. Even in summer, the high moors and valleys could not escape chill.

Did she imagine that a smile appeared in the shadows of his cowl?

"I believe I understand their methods. I would have done the same were I them. As would Merlin himself." Hawkwood spoke slowly. "And

I believe there is a way that Merlin would have countered those actions. Return to Magnus, but this time, visit Thomas so you can become close to him."

"Is he to see my face?"

"Not yet. Let's first wait to see if he can defeat the Earl of York. We'll both return to Magnus. We have to get inside before the siege begins. Me as the herbalist he already knows, and you as the Katherine he remembers. You do have your mask?"

She held out a small travel bag as an answer.

With practiced movements, she flipped her hair upward and pushed the long tail into a flat bundle against her head and held it there as she wrapped the cloth around her jaws, then her nose and eyes and forehead.

When she finished, only a large black hole for her mouth and two dark narrow slits for her eyes showed any degree of humanity. It was time for Katherine, the scarred freak and friend of Thomas, to return to Magnus.

THIRTY-SEVEN

From the ramparts of the castle, Thomas and Robert watched the faraway blur of banners and horses as the front of the army approached. The mass of men and beasts was plain to see as it wound its way through the valley.

The sounds of that army drifted upward to them. Grunting beasts. The slap of leather against ground as men marched in unison. And the rise of voices below Thomas and Robert as villagers heard of the army's progress.

"Anywhere else," Robert said, "and I would advise immediate surrender. But there's a reason Magnus has survived all through the centuries."

"I know I can depend on the castle walls and the moat," Thomas said. "But Magnus will not stand unless the soldiers fight for me and the villagers support the soldiers."

Robert put a hand on Thomas's shoulder. "But you are well trusted, m'lord. While there are whispers of dissent among the people, as to be expected, the soldiers still are loyal to you."

"That's good to hear."

Robert opened his mouth as if to speak, then closed it again.

Thomas smiled. "Out with it."

"There has been talk, however, and much speculation."

"Yes?" Thomas asked.

"Nobody knows why the earl has declared war. They wonder how you might have offended him to drive him to battle."

Thomas lost his smile. "That is something I wish I knew."

They watched in silence for long minutes.

When the army reached the narrow bridge of land that connected the island fortress to the land around the lake, one man, on foot, detached himself from the front of the army.

Thomas watched briefly, then spoke more to himself than to Robert as the man, alone, walked slowly toward the castle.

"He holds paper rolled and sealed. I have little faith the message is a greeting of friendship."

THIRTY-EIGHT

Katherine woke in the gutter to hands reaching roughly within her blanket. Sour breath, heavy garlic, and the odor of unwashed skin pressed down.

Katherine almost screamed in rage, then remembered her role—burned and scarred too horribly to deserve any form of kindness.

Her voice became a low begging moan instead.

"Awake? Bad luck for you!" From the darkness, a broad hand loomed to block out the light of the stars, and the blow that followed shot white flashes through her closed eyes. Her left cheek swelled immediately tight beneath the bandages.

Katherine bit back a yelp of pain and resigned herself to being robbed of what little she owned.

Another voice interrupted the figure above her.

"My good man," it called cheerfully from just down the street, "you show kindness to assist strangers during this dangerous time of night. Here, now, let me help you get this poor woman from the gutters."

"Eh?"

The voice from behind its candle moved closer. "And probably not a moment too soon. Why, any common gutter thief might have swooped in like a pest-ridden vulture. And then where would this poor woman be without our help?"

The startled man above Katherine swore under his breath, then fled.

She drew herself upright into a sitting position and hugged her knees. Through the narrow slits of the constricting bandages, it was difficult to see her rescuer as he approached. It was easy, however, to hear his warm chuckle.

"Like a rat scurrying away from a torch. And without a shred of good humor."

The candle flared and moved downward with the man's slow, stooping motion. Katherine, still wrapped and hidden in a thin blanket, flinched at his touch.

"Come, my child," the voice. "I am one of several town guards, under hire to the lord of Magnus himself. I mean you no harm. I will bring you to the church where you will be fed and kept warm."

"I have no money," Katherine replied. "Surely that must be obvious at my choice of accommodation."

Another warm chuckle. "You are a stranger here."

"No, I—"

"Otherwise, you would know the lord of Magnus provides a generous allowance to the church for the purpose of sheltering those in need who are willing to work in exchange for the shelter."

His hand found her elbow and guided her to her feet.

She could not see his face behind the candle. But she heard his gasp as he pushed aside the blanket that covered her face.

That familiar sound tore at her heart. It reminded her again of the nightmare of living the life of a freak. Freedom from that life— traveling with the old man and watching the joy in Thomas's eyes as he drank in the youth and beauty of her uncovered face—had been so precious after years imprisoned beneath the filthy bandages. And for a moment, she could not sponge away bitterness inside.

"Horror?" she mocked his gasp. "You were expecting an angel, perhaps?"

Long silence. Then words she would never forget. "Not horror, my child. Surprised relief. Thomas of Magnus has spoken to many, and often, of his friend Katherine. It will give him great joy to see you."

⚜

Katherine woke again to the touch of hands. These ones, however, were gentle, and plucked at the bandages on her face.

"No!" Her terror was real—not acted, as so much of her life beneath bandages had been.

The servant woman misunderstood the reason for that terror.

"Shh, my child. Thomas has instructed you be bathed and given fresh wraps and new clothing."

"No!" Katherine clutched the servant woman's wrists. "My face!"

"Hush, little one. You shall not be mocked in the lord's home."

Katherine did not have time to appreciate the irony—after a lifetime of abuse, kindness itself finally threatened the secrecy of her disguise. Should those of the darkness discover she had been among them all these years…

Katherine pushed herself into an upright position. "Please. Lead me to the bath. Leave the fresh wrap nearby. But I beg of you, grant me the solace of privacy. To inflict my face upon others…"

"Of course," the servant woman said softly.

Katherine let strong, calloused hands guide her from the warmth of the bed. Before she could barely notice the coldness of the floor, the servant woman stooped and fitted on her feet slippers of sheepskin.

As Katherine relaxed and turned to accept help into the offered robe, she smothered a cry of delighted surprise. The previous night had been too dark for her to see her new sleeping quarters in the castle. What she saw explained why sleep had been so sound.

Her bed was huge, and canopied with veils of netting. Her mattress of straw—what luxury!—hung from the canopy on rope suspenders. The mattress was covered with linen sheets, and blankets of wool and fur. Feather-stuffed pillows too!

Such softness of sleep. Such softness of the robe against her skin. Katherine suddenly became uncomfortably aware of her filth and how she did not belong in a room like this. Her arms and legs were smeared with grease and dirt. The pile of clothes beside her was little more than torn rags. And, in the cool freshness of the room, she suddenly became aware of the stink of the streets upon her body.

She faltered slightly.

The servant woman ignored that.

"Come, m'lady," the woman said. "Your bath awaits. And you shall greet Thomas of Magnus like a queen."

THIRTY-NINE

He appears so serious, Katherine thought. *Already, the weight of his power bends him.*

So she began with an awkward bow. As her heart thudded, she wondered in anguish, knowing she could never ask. *Does he feel for me the way I do for him? Or did my wishful imagination deceive me during those few moments he stared at me beneath the moonlight?*

Katherine forced herself to remember she was beneath bandages—not a midnight messenger—and began to speak as she finished her curtsy. "You overwhelm me with these gifts of…"

Thomas frowned and shook his head slightly.

Katherine stopped.

Thomas stared straight ahead, every inch of his seated body the ruler of Magnus. Behind Katherine, each side of the huge double wooden door slowly swung closed under the guidance of the sentries just outside the room.

The doors thudded shut.

Thomas let out a great sigh.

"They seem to prefer it when I am solemn," he said with a slight smile. "And with the Earl of York determined to take Magnus, it is not difficult to appear that way. I'm glad, however, to see you."

Thomas stepped down lightly.

"Katherine, you've returned." He knelt, took one of her hands, and kissed the back of it. He stood and placed both his hands on her shoulders. "I've missed our conversations."

Katherine smiled beneath her bandages. *He goes from formidable man to a sweet boyishness in such a short time. Not bragging about the Valley of Surrender. Not boasting of his new wealth. But spending effort setting me—a person he believes to be a freak—at ease. It would not be difficult to remain in love with such a person.*

She, of course, kept those thoughts to herself. Instead, she replied, "Thank you, m'lord."

"M'lord! Not 'Thomas'? After you rescued me from the dungeon? After you made it possible to conquer the walls of Magnus? You gravely disappoint me with such an insult."

Grave disappointment, however, did not show on his face. Only warmth.

Would that I could tear these bandages from my face, Katherine thought. *Only to watch his eyes and hope he smiles to recognize me from my visit to his tent at the army camp.*

She tried to keep the conversation safe so nothing in her actions might betray her thoughts. So her questions would reflect ignorance. "How fares that rascal Tiny John? Or the knight Sir William?"

A complex expression crossed Thomas's face—a mixture of frown and smile. She soon understood why.

"Tiny John still entertains us all," Thomas told her as the smile triumphed briefly, then lost to the frown and his eyes darkened. "The knight bade farewell much too soon after Magnus was conquered. There was much about him that cannot be explained."

He tried a half smile in her direction. "Much, also, is a mystery to me here in Magnus. I feel there is no one here I can trust."

He looked at her strangely. "Even your disappearance the night we conquered Magnus…"

Katherine bowed her head. "Thomas—"

"No," he said as if coming to a quick decision. "I was not seeking an explanation. You, more than anyone, assisted me to this lordship. I am happy that you have returned. Furthermore, urgent matters press upon me."

"Oh?"

"Strange evil generated by an ancient circle of high priests known as Druids. And worse."

Thomas stared into space. "As you know," he said, "when I first arrived in Magnus, the former lord, Richard Mewburn, had me arrested and thrown into the dungeon because of the deaths of three monks. My explanation to you was truth. One was bludgeoned by the other, and the remaining two killed themselves by accidently eating the food meant for me, food they had poisoned to murder me."

Katherine nodded.

Thomas responded to her nod by starting to pace back and forth across the room, brows furrowed, hands clenched behind his back, and royal purple cloak across broad shoulders.

"After Mewburn fled in defeat," he continued while pacing, "all in Magnus accepted that the charges of murder had been false, merely an excuse to imprison me and the knight."

Katherine nodded again.

"Yet today," Thomas said, "I received a message from the Earl of York that he has sworn an oath of justice, that he is determined to overthrow Magnus and imprison me for those same murders. There was enough time during the march to the battle against the Scots for the

Earl of York to accuse me of murder. There was enough time then for him to arrest me. Why did he not?"

"Perhaps because the time is convenient for him now that his son is no longer a hostage in your castle?" Katherine suggested.

Thomas glanced at her briefly, then shook off a strange expression.

"There is also that matter," he said a moment later. "He says he demands revenge for what I did to his son. This on the heels of a message I sent to him, telling him that his son broke honor by fleeing from my castle. It's as if the earl is determined to find an excuse to take Magnus."

Long silence.

"Had the Earl of York heard of the deaths before the march?" Katherine started.

"That is what puzzles me. If so, why suddenly decide to act upon them later?" Thomas stopped pacing and stared directly at Katherine.

"However," he said, "the monastery of my childhood was obscure, and I as an orphan, more so. Thus, it is easier to think that the Earl of York had not heard of the deaths."

Thomas frowned, "How, then, did Mewburn, the former lord of Magnus—here in the isolated moors—know of those deaths soon enough to cast me into the dungeon, while others in power, such as the Earl of York, remained uninformed until much later?"

"I wish I could answer that for you," Katherine said.

Thomas gripped the edge of the stone as he leaned forward. "I am not without hope." He turned to her. "I am going to be gone for a day. Please don't worry about my absence."

"You're leaving Magnus? How? It is impossible. We are under siege."

"At night," he said. "On the water."

"Where are you going?"

"Some things," he said, "I can't share with anybody."

FORTY

Thomas was on a hillside, miles from Magnus. He had carefully hidden himself in thick brush, where a gap in the branches allowed sunlight.

He was hot and thirsty, and too often ants crawled up the outside of his clothing and onto his hands, but he dared not sit anywhere else.

Not with the single book in his lap.

There were others, wrapped carefully in oiled leather and hidden in a pile of rocks, but he only allowed himself to take one book at a time from the small collection.

If, somehow, he were caught or trapped, then all he would lose was a single book. Unthinkable enough that he might lose the others in his collection, but totally unfathomable that he would risk his entire library.

As for whether a man might be murdered to steal a book from him, that, too, was a possibility. It didn't matter that the thief would more than likely be illiterate; when a book might take a year to be hand copied by a monk, any book was valuable merely for the labor put into it.

Thomas's books had far more value, however, for the knowledge contained in each.

On the hillside, not for the first time did he wish earnestly that he had his entire library to consult. But it had been impossible to travel with them on his journey to conquer Magnus, when his only companions were those who had been condemned to hang before he helped them escape. Physically, to travel with the books would have required a horse and a cart, something that would have drawn too much attention to their escape.

After becoming lord of Magnus, it had still been too risky to move his library. The appearance of Isabelle had proven that. He was watched—somehow—too closely at Magnus. How could he successfully bring the books in and keep them a secret? And where could he keep the books and trust they would be safe?

The only alternative had been to make his way back to the cave near the abbey where the books truly were safe, and smuggle the most important ones almost back to Magnus, where he could reach them, like now, in under a day's travel.

He had never expected, of course, that all of Magnus would be surrounded by an army, that he would have to find a way outside of the village walls and off the island to reach the books.

Thomas pinched another ant that had made it past his boot, hardly aware he was doing it.

The book in his lap gave no satisfaction, no suggestions on how to defeat the earl.

He'd have to slowly go back to the pile of rocks, wrap this book, unwrap another, then sneak back to this hiding spot and hope to learn something from that book to help him keep Magnus.

And, if somehow he found a solution, he'd need to survive the trip back to Magnus.

❧

With his hand on a large, flat piece of floating lumber, Thomas stood waist-deep in water and reeds beneath a moonless sky, knowing he had failed. He was returning to Magnus without any plan for how to stop the Earl of York's siege or how to defeat the Druids. Either opponent alone at this point appeared on the verge of victory; to face both of them and expect to keep Magnus was impossible.

As the small waves of the lake lapped up against his legs, it struck Thomas that if he were strictly a rational being, he would step back out of the water and flee the valley.

He had no family ties to keep him in Magnus, and certainly the property that was his was about to be taken away. Far away, at the abbey, he'd stored gold coin that would make his life easy for years.

If he walked out of the lake at this moment and returned to the abbey, he'd have his library of knowledge, a small fortune, and the freedom to go anywhere in Britain and start a life of his own. He could lie about his past and begin as a young merchant. Or he could become a soldier.

That was the decision a rational being would make.

It was utterly irrational that he would attempt to return to Magnus, hoping Robert had not used the authority bestowed upon him to open the gates to the Earl of York and negotiate a treaty that would leave Robert as lord of Magnus.

It was utterly irrational that Thomas would swallow his fear of the deep waters ahead and paddle in the dark, clinging to a plank for flotation.

It was utterly irrational to choose to accept his role as a lord of a small kingdom of people who were openly speaking against him, believers of dark superstitions who chose to accept that Thomas had been cursed.

So why was he pushing forward, the water now at his chest?

Ahead, he'd have to kick his legs for an hour to propel the plank forward, trusting that in the dark of night on the dark of the water, he would not be seen by any sentries of the earl's army, trusting that Robert would be waiting on the island at the appointed hour, not with a sword to end Thomas's life, but with an extended hand to pull Thomas onto land, with the keys to a door that would let them back into the safety of the walls.

The land fell away from his feet, and Thomas slowly kicked forward, trying not to think about the depths of the water ahead of him.

Really, he should turn back and leave Magnus to its fate. Both the Druids and the earl had promised him a horrible death.

Still, he kicked forward, with his body weight from the waist forward on the plank.

He did not know how to win back his kingdom, nor did he even expect it would happen.

But he could not quit.

Because a life as a coward was, to him, a far worse fate than whatever was ahead.

FORTY-ONE

Katherine, her face hidden in bandages, joined Thomas along the top of the walls.

"It is impressive in a horrible way," she observed. "Why is it in man's nature to be so cruel to other men?"

Even with distance across the water that provided a buffer from the opposing soldiers, Thomas could see they were well armed. Battle-axes, longbows, war hammers, maces, crossbows, lances, and pikes were all in plain sight.

Larger war machines were in already in place; Thomas counted three trebuchets at the beginning stages of construction. These massive levers with attached slings were far too big to transport and had to be built at the siege site. Each would be able to hurl a stone of up to two hundred pounds toward the castle from a distance of three hundred yards.

"I presume you didn't expect an answer to your question," Thomas said. "As for the horrible impressiveness, I have to agree."

"Does it frighten you?"

"Not the army. Or the weapons. Magnus could be safe even if the earl doubles the army and weapons. It has survived similar sieges in the past."

Thomas was not presenting a brave face to encourage her. He knew the earl's weapons posed little danger. The entire village, with its thick perimeter walls, was on the island. The castle itself towered above all. The lake, however, was its best defense. Because the trebuchets could not get close enough to hurl stones heavy enough to batter the stone walls of the castle, the defenders would be facing lighter stones that would simply be a nuisance and distraction.

"He's doing this for appearance, isn't he," Katherine said.

"That is what I fear. The whispers among the people are increasing. They still speak of the bats that fell from the sky in daylight. If the dissent spreads to my soldiers, I am lost. It's sloppy to leave all those weapons lying about, and his soldiers are anything but sloppy. My guess is they have orders to leave them in plain sight so the villagers get a good look. He's hoping that if he frightens them enough, I'll face a revolt inside the walls. That's the only way to conquer Magnus, as we have food and water enough to last ten years."

⚜

Katherine ached to tell Thomas more, to tell him he was not alone in his struggle against the Druids. But she could not. Hawkwood's remembered warning echoed stronger than the inner voice that begged her to remove the bandages from her face.

She needed again to speak to Hawkwood.

"Did your absence help?" she asked.

Thomas shook his head. "I don't know where to turn."

"Whom do you trust?" Katherine asked several minutes later. "Robert of Uleran?"

"His dismay at the escape of the prisoner in my absence seemed real," Thomas said. "Upon my return, he offered his resignation. Now…now I have no other choice but to trust him. After the unnatural happenings, his open loyalty is a bedrock that keeps many of the super-stitious soldiers faithful to our cause."

She had nothing more to say, and she wanted only to place her hand on his arm.

⚜

Thomas stared with rigid anger at the encircling army. He was remembering his conversation with the mysterious woman who had bound him with rope and spoken to him on the hillside while he was blindfolded and completely powerless.

"All I want for myself is to remain lord of Magnus," he'd told her. *"I have no interest in choosing sides in some battle you pretend is so important. I need no help and will remain lord of Magnus by my own wits and willpower."*

"Katherine," he said. "I finally realize that if I rely only upon myself, I have no hope. I need help, and I would be prepared to take it if somehow I knew where to go to ask for it."

FORTY-TWO

Katherine found Hawkwood with a bowl of porridge in his hands, sitting at an inn table.

As the herbalist from the other valley, he'd been trapped, as all around him knew, by the suddenness of the siege. Nobody questioned his presence in Magnus.

And because Katherine was long known among the people as the girl whose face had been scarred by fire, nobody gave notice as she sat at the table with her own bowl of porridge.

"I have a toothache," she said loudly for the benefit of anyone overly interested in their conversation.

"John's wort, then," he answered. "Follow me."

She did.

Outside, in the sunshine, they had privacy.

"Do you have news of Thomas?" Hawkwood asked.

"He was gone all day yesterday. In the castle, servants were wondering if he had somehow fled Magnus, not to return. But this morning, he is back."

"I fear Thomas is in grave danger," Hawkwood said. "As you can imagine, I hear every rumor and whisper. The talk is that Thomas is cursed, and that to remove the curse upon Magnus, Thomas must be removed. Has he spoken to you of any plans to defeat the Earl of York?"

"None," she answered. "But we can take comfort in knowing that he has defied the Druids, can we not?"

Hawkwood shook his head. "This is a cat-and-mouse game, Katherine. It would serve them well to have him pretend defiance in an effort to draw us out. After all, the earl has merely surrounded the castle, but has yet to openly attack. Our greatest protection is that we are as invisible to them as they are invisible to us. We will know Thomas's true allegiance when he gives up his greatest secret."

"As you know, he told me he was prepared to accept help."

"That, as I told you before, makes me wonder if it is part of a game. For by telling you, does that mean he suspects the bandages across your face are a disguise?"

"Perhaps we should go one step further. Perhaps I should reveal myself."

"Is that your heart speaking?"

She didn't answer.

"Remember, Katherine, we cannot assume he will join us."

"But if he loses Magnus," Katherine said, "it will matter little where he becomes an Immortal. We need both: his books and the castle."

Hawkwood nodded, gray hair falling across his face.

"I don't see that we have any choice," Hawkwood said. "It is time for you to help him defeat the earl. But you must remain hidden beneath your bandages. He is not to know you are my messenger."

Katherine hoped she was able to hide disappointment. Someday, she wanted to be able to speak to Thomas not as a hideous freak, but as the woman who wanted his love and wanted to return it.

homas found what he was looking for in an alley behind the small stone church: a dog, barely more than a puppy. It had short dark hair, with ribs that gleamed behind fur that looked like a worn piece of clothing.

On his knees, Thomas coaxed it forward by holding out a piece of raw beef. It shivered with delight and shyness at his attention, wagging its tail frantically and whining as it slowly moved toward Thomas's hand.

"There's a good boy," Thomas said. "Come on. Come on."

The dog moved close enough to make a quick snap for the piece of meat. Thomas didn't let go.

Briefly, there was a tug of war, and as the dog strained to pull the meat loose, Thomas reached with his other hand and wrapped his arm under the dog's chest, behind its front legs.

With a secure grip on the dog, Thomas released the meat. The dog gobbled it as Thomas lifted the dog off the ground. The dog kicked and squirmed but did not try to bite him.

He scratched the dog's head and made comforting sounds to it as he carried it through the village, aware of puzzled looks from people as he passed them on the streets.

He ignored the puzzled looks, which, at least, were better than seeing people furtively make the sign of the cross as they saw him, trying to ward off the curse that they feared might touch them too.

It only took minutes to return to the castle. He made no explanations to the guards as he marched through the corridors.

Gradually, as he'd been walking, the dog had squirmed less and less, until, as Thomas reached his bedchamber on the upper floor of the castle, the dog was relaxed and motionless, as if asleep.

Thomas knew better.

He'd added a poison to the meat. For all the risk he'd taken to swim across the lake at night to spend a day with his books and swim back again the following night, he'd learned nothing to help him in a battle against the siege of the Earl of York.

However, there'd been a long section of one of the books that dealt with medicinal herbs and roots, and he'd learned something that interested him so greatly that he'd spent a couple of hours preparing the potion that served as a poison.

Thomas had already set a blanket on the stone floor, near the fireplace. He placed the dog on the blanket.

He stared closely at the dog's ribs and watched the rhythm of movement. Unconscious, not asleep, the dog's breaths came slower and further apart, until finally, the ribs stopped all movement.

Thomas leaned down and placed his head on the dog's chest. The heartbeat, barely audible, disappeared altogether.

Thomas lifted the dog's lower lip away from its jaws, and pinched the tender, moist skin, applying so much pressure that he broke the skin.

The dog didn't react. He'd succeeded.

There was no denying all the symptoms of death. He waited until the dog recovered, something that would have seemed like a miracle had he not known about the potion. And finally, he was certain.

That left him his second task, one that would not be near as simple or easy to accomplish. Facing the Earl of York.

FORTY-FOUR

Thomas and Robert of Uleran stood and waited at the end of the drawbridge.

At the other end of the narrow strip of land that reached the shore of the lake, the Earl of York and three soldiers began to move toward them.

"Are you sure they'll not run us through with those great swords?" Robert asked.

"The earl will not risk losing honor by dealing treachery," Thomas said.

Thomas and Robert of Uleran stared straight ahead. Each wore a long cloak of the finest material in Magnus—it was not a time to appear humble or afraid.

The Earl of York's march across the land bridge seemed to take forever. When he was close enough, Thomas observed the anger set in the clenched muscles of his face.

He heard that anger moments later.

"What is it you want, you craven cur of yellow cowardice?" the earl snarled.

"An explanation perhaps, of this sudden hatred," Thomas said shortly. "I understand—if you truly believe me guilty of those murders—that duty forces you to lay siege. But you once called me brother. Surely that—"

"Treacherous vulture. Waste no charm on me," the earl said in thunderous tones. "Were it not for honor, I would cleave you in two where you stand. You called me here for discussion. Do it quickly, so that I may refuse your request and return to the important matter of bringing destruction to Magnus. After that, I shall serve you for dinner the ear you sent back to me."

"Ear?" Thomas stiffened visibly, though he kept his voice level and polite.

"The one you cut off the head of my son. Don't pretend innocence with me."

"I promise," Thomas said, "I have no idea what you are talking about."

The earl threw down a piece of paper.

Robert picked it up and handed it to Thomas, who glanced at it and saw enough to begin to understand why the earl was outraged.

…I will only agree to a pact of allegiance once I receive a payment of gold for my services during the march against the Scots. Ensure that it completely fills the chest I have sent back with your son. If it does not arrive within a fortnight, I will consider your inaction to be a declaration of war. As proof of the seriousness of my intent to wage battle against you if you do not send the gold, look no further than the ear I have taken from your son.

"That is not my handwriting," Thomas said. "I would be happy to show you other correspondence from my quill."

"It had your royal seal."

"Fraud does happen. If someone wanted to set us against each other, it would be easy to arrange."

"And my son would partake in this fraud?"

"I cannot speak for him."

"And lose his ear?" the earl asked.

"I cannot speak for him," Thomas repeated. "I can only tell you the truth that I know. I did not cut off his ear. He had escaped from Magnus shortly before I returned from war."

Thomas gazed levelly at the earl. "Those of the symbol asked me to join them. I refused. Perhaps this is a result of that."

The earl took a deep breath, as if seriously considering Thomas's innocence for the first time.

"I cannot turn back," the earl said. Almost regretfully. "In front of the world, I have committed to battle against you."

"I ask, then, for a chance to prove my innocence."

"Surrender the castle then. Submit to a trial. You have my word I will do my best to prove the message delivered to me did not come from your hand."

Thomas shook his head. "I ask for trial by ordeal."

The Earl of York gaped at him. "Ordeal!"

That, too, had been Thomas's reaction to instructions placed beneath his pillow, ensuring that only he would discover them the evening before as he prepared for sleep in his bedchamber.

"Ordeal!" the Earl of York repeated, showing for the first time an emotion other than anger. "The church outlawed such trials more than a hundred years ago."

"Nonetheless," Thomas said, "I wish to prove to you, and to the people of Magnus, that I am innocent."

The earl rubbed his chin in thought. "Tell me, shall we bind you and throw you into the lake?"

That had been, as Thomas knew, one of the most common ways of establishing guilt. Bound, and often weighted with stones, a person was thrown into deep water. If he or she floated, it proved witchcraft. If the accused drowned, it proved innocence.

"Not by water," Thomas said. "Nor by fire."

Some chose the hot iron. The defendant was forced to pick up an iron weight, still glowing from the forge. If, after three days in bandages, the burns had healed, it was taken as a sign of innocence.

"What then?" the Earl of York demanded. "How are we to believe you are innocent? You are going to propose your own trial by ordeal? This isn't done."

"If you allow it, then it is done."

"What do you suggest?"

"Tomorrow, I will stand alone on this narrow strip of land," Thomas said. "Stampede toward me twenty of the strongest and largest bulls you can find. If I turn and run, or if I am crushed and trampled, then you may have Magnus."

FORTY-FIVE

The wrinkles in Gervaise's face—as for all people at a certain age—reflected the expression that had been dominant on his face over all the years. For Gervaise, the usual set of his face was a quizzical friendliness that gave him the look of a parent who was tolerant and pleased with a young child.

Now, however, his brows were furrowed with concern. He held a white cross made of painted wood, resting the base of it on the stone floor of the church. The top of the cross reached his chest.

To Thomas, this humble and gentle man far better represented the Christ of the gospels than any priest or monk he had known.

Thomas was all too aware of how some churches were huge and grandiose, built on the money taken from peasants who were starved and often in desperate need of comfort.

Thomas was aware that, because the church only allowed a Latin version of the Bible, a priest could twist any passage to suit his own goals and desires, while the sheep of the congregation had no way of knowing if the sermon reflected what was truly in the Bible.

Thomas was aware that men often joined the priesthood because it paid well, and more importantly, gave them immunity from prosecution for any number of crimes. Yes, a priest could literally get away with murder.

Thomas was aware of the abuses he'd faced in his own past from men who claimed to be godly. He believed he had good reason to be suspicious of anything related to the church.

Thomas particularly liked something that Gervaise often said about the New Testament—all it took for a man or woman to be reconciled with God was to ask for forgiveness.

This was not what the priests taught. They claimed that a man or woman must earn a passage to heaven by donating money to the church. Indeed, the sale of indulgences was brisk business in the church across Europe; people could give money to the church to rescue dead loved ones from the clutches of hell, or purchase their own eternal salvation. Or worse, guarantee eternal damnation by not purchasing an indulgence.

Gervaise, on the other hand, was fond of quoting a passage from the gospel of John the apostle, telling his own flock that God so loved the world that He'd given His only Son, that whoever believed in this Son would be given eternal life.

Where then, the need to earn forgiveness or give money to the church for salvation? Such simplicity made Gervaise a threat to the church coffers. Thomas had earlier decided that if ever the priest tried to remove Gervaise, he would do everything in his power to protect the man.

Of course, it did not look as though Thomas would retain his power as lord of Magnus much longer.

"I wanted us to talk," Gervaise said, lifting the cross and extending it to Thomas, "because I hope you will take this when you face the bulls."

"In a sense I'm disappointed," Thomas answered. "We both know it is a powerful symbol, and your motives are easy to guess. If I succeed, you want all of Magnus to believe it is because of the church."

"Not the church," Gervaise said. "Our heavenly Father. A church is only a building and a religious structure created by man to help bring all of us to our heavenly Father."

"You know the people won't see it that way. If I carry the cross, it will be a clear statement that my allegiance is to the church. I'm surprised that you would play politics like this. I would have expected the priest to ask of me such a favor, but not you, not after all you've done to lead me to faith in the Christ of the gospels."

"Hardly," Gervaise said without taking insult or showing irritation. "If I were a political man, the last thing I would want is for you to carry the cross. For a political man would be convinced that the bulls will trample you to death, and a political man would not want your foolish, horrible fate blamed on the cross. After all, if you hold the cross and you die, it will look like the cross was incapable of protecting you."

Thomas was forced to agree, and he nodded before speaking again. "I am no longer disappointed, then, but curious. Why would you want to take this risk and have me carry the cross?"

"I don't see it as a risk," Gervaise said. "While I completely believe that our heavenly Father has the power to protect through miraculous means, I'm also convinced that you are not expecting to need His protection. After all, in all our discussions, you have expressed a degree of skepticism and a reluctance to share the faith. I suspect you have some earthly power you intend to use. I'm convinced you will survive trial by ordeal."

"Is this all you wanted to ask me, whether I would carry the cross? If so, I must take leave."

Gervaise laughed. "Your lack of trust is easy to see, Thomas. I understand it completely. After all, if you revealed to me what you have planned, and I in turn share it with others, then even if you survive the running of the bulls, your bold gamble will fail. For none will believe it was a supernatural event."

"As I said," Thomas replied, "if this is all you intended to discuss, I must go and ready myself for what lies ahead."

"Please listen," Gervaise said. "I think it's important that you take the cross. Not because of what the church might gain from your gamble, but because of what you will gain as lord of Magnus."

"I'm listening."

"It is clear that the people of Magnus ascribe the supernatural sign of the bats falling as dark forces gathered against you, and whispers of Druids are becoming louder and louder. It is obvious to me that you can only hold your kingdom by defeating or appearing to defeat these signs. In other words, if superstition among the people is leading dangerously close to the loss of your kingdom, then you have decided that superstition among the people is also a way to lead them back to you. It is a two-edged sword, is it not?"

"It is."

"Lay down that sword, Thomas. Because in the end, you are simply giving more strength to superstition, and eventually, the other edge of the sword may triumph. Instead, you can use this opportunity to damage the power of superstition."

"Ah," Thomas said. "If it looks like the cross can defeat superstition, then the people will remain within the fold of the church and lose their fear of Druids."

"In plain words, yes."

"Isn't that a dangerous game for you? After all, if I succeed through earthly powers, then the power of the cross is merely a sham."

Gervaise spoke earnestly. "Thomas, there is nothing sham about faith in our heavenly Father. I believe He is protecting you by providing what you need to succeed. I ask you to examine the teachings of the Son of the heavenly Father as shown in the four gospels. Wouldn't it be much better for Magnus if its people followed His example, instead of fearing Druids? I ask of you, give careful consideration, for much is at stake here."

"I need give it no further consideration," Thomas said. He reached for the cross. "You have indeed given me wise advice."

FORTY-SIX

Katherine stood among the great crowd at the base of the castle. For once, she was almost grateful for the bandages around her face. They hid her ironic smile to notice the stale sweat stench of the men and women hemmed against her—several days of castle living had spoiled her.

She was in the crowd because she wanted to hear and watch Thomas, and there was no way for her to remain beside him as he addressed the people from the top of the castle stairs.

When he appeared, the rustling undercurrents of speculation immediately stopped. Thomas held complete attention.

Once again, Katherine was grateful for the bandages. The new smile was one of admiration. She wasn't sure she would have wanted Thomas to know he impressed her. Not if his feelings for her were different than her feelings for him.

"People of Magnus," Thomas began, "today I face death."

Whispers and excited chattering.

Thomas held up his hand for silence. He wore only simple clothes. A brown cloak. No jewelry. In his arms, he carried the white cross Gervaise had built.

"Because of you I undergo trial by ordeal. Magnus can withstand any siege, but only with your support. Some of you have chosen to believe I am guilty of the charges laid against me. Today, then, I prove my innocence so that Magnus might stand. I tell you now, God will cause dogs to howl and bats to fall from the sky at the injustice of false accusations."

Thomas said nothing more. He spun on his heel and marched back into the castle.

⚜

Surely he feels fear.

From Katherine's viewpoint among the hundreds of men and women of Magnus lined along the top of the fortress wall, Thomas appeared small and lost, standing alone halfway across the land bridge. He held the white cross in front of him.

Thomas stood completely still and faced the opposing army. Between them, and where the land bridge joined the shore of the lake, a hastily constructed pen—made from logs roped together—held huge and restless bulls. From the castle wall, they seemed dark and evil.

Katherine frowned. Why a heap of dried bushes at the back end of that pen?

The collective tension of the spectators began to fill her too.

Soldiers moved to the front of the pen.

A sigh from the crowd along the fortress wall, like the wind that swept down the valley hills across them.

Thomas crossed his arms and moved his feet apart slightly, as if bracing himself.

If he turns and runs, he declares his guilt. Yet how can he remain there as the bulls charge? The land is too narrow. Surely he will be crushed.

A sudden muttering took Katherine from her thoughts. She looked beyond Thomas, and understood immediately.

The bushes at the rear of the pen...soldiers with torches... They meant to drive the bulls into a frenzy with fire! Thomas had not agreed to this!

The vulnerable figure that was Thomas remained planted. Katherine fought tears.

Within moments, the dried brush crackled, and high flames were plain to see from the castle walls.

Bellows of rage filled the air as the massive bulls began to push forward against the gate. Monstrous black silhouettes rose from the rear and struggled to climb over those in front as the fire surged higher and higher.

Then, just as the pen itself bulged outward from the strain of tons upon tons of heavy muscle in panic, the soldiers slashed the rope that held the gate shut.

Bulls exploded forward toward Thomas in a massed charge.

Fifty yards away, he waited.

Does he cry for help? Katherine could not watch. Neither could she close her eyes. Not with the thunder that pounded the earth. Not with the bellowed terror and fury and roar of violence of churning hooves and razor-sharp horns bearing down on him like a black storm of hatred.

Thirty-five yards away, Thomas waited.

Men and women around Katherine began to scream.

Still, he did not move.

Twenty-five yards. Then twenty.

One more heartbeat and the gap had closed to fifteen yards.

Screams grew louder.

Then the unbelievable.

The lead bulls swerved, then plunged into the water on either side of Thomas. Within moments, even as the bellows of rage drowned out the screams atop the castle walls, the bulls parted as they threw themselves away from the tiny figure in front of them.

Katherine slumped.

It was over.

No bull remained on land. Each swam strongly for the nearest shore.

Another sigh from the crowd atop the castle walls. But before excited talk could begin, the first of the bulls reached the shore of the lake. As it landed and took its first steps, it roared with renewed rage and bolted away from the cautiously approaching soldiers.

Small saplings snapped as it charged and bucked and bellowed through the trees lining the shore, through the tents and campfires, and finally to the open land beyond.

Each bull did the same as it reached land, and soldiers fled in all directions.

And behind the people, dogs started to howl in the streets. The men and women of Magnus turned in time to see bats swooping and rising in panic in bright sunshine, until moments later, the first one fell to earth.

FORTY-SEVEN

K atherine did not see Thomas anywhere on the streets of Magnus during the celebration that traditionally followed the end of a siege. Merchants and shopkeepers, normally cheap to the point of meanness, poured wine for the lowliest of peasants and shared the best cakes and freshest meats freely.

Around her was joyful song—much of it off-tune because of the wine—and the vibrant plucked tunes of six-stringed lutes and the jangle of tambourines.

People, even the most bitter of neighbors, danced and hugged one another as long-lost brothers. Today, the threat of death had vanished, and their lord, Thomas of Magnus, had been proven innocent. How could they have ever doubted after the uncanny howling of dogs and the death of bats that had followed Thomas's trial by ordeal?

Katherine moved aimlessly from street to street. Never, of course, in her life as a freak in Magnus, had she felt she belonged. This celebration was no different. Few offered her cakes, few offered her wine, and no one took her hand to dance.

Did it matter? she wondered. All those years of loneliness, years served as duty for a greater cause. She thought she had become accustomed to the cruelty of people who judged merely by appearance.

Yet today, the pain drove past the cold walls around her heart. Because of Thomas. Because she could remember not wearing the bandages. Like a bird freed from its cage, then imprisoned once more, she longed to fly again.

Now, walking along the streets and among the crowds, thinking of Thomas darkened her usual loneliness.

Yes, Thomas had proven his courage. Yes, Thomas had defeated the Druid attempt at rebellion within Magnus. And yes, Thomas had also turned away the most powerful earl in the north.

But the Druids had not been completely conquered. Magnus was not free from danger.

Katherine frowned beneath her bandages. She was disappointed in her own selfishness. So much was at stake. Her duty to Hawkwood proved it day after day. Yet she could barely look beyond her feelings— a frustrating ache—and beyond the insane desire to rip from her face the bandages that hid her from Thomas.

She sighed, remembering Hawkwood's instructions. *"Until we are certain which side he has chosen, he cannot know of you, or of the rest of us. The stakes are far too great. We risk your presence back in Magnus for the sole reason that—despite all we've done—he is or might become one of them. Love cannot cloud your judgment of the situation."*

Head down and lost in her thoughts, Katherine did not see Gervaise until he clapped a friendly hand upon her shoulder.

"Dear friend," he said, "Thomas wishes you to join him."

FORTY-EIGHT

The Roman caltrops worked as predicted," Thomas said as greeting. He stood beside the large chair in his throne room and did not even wait for the guard to completely close the large doors. A small dog was curled on the ground at his feet.

Strange. Thomas trusts me enough to reveal how he survived the charge of the bulls?

Katherine kept her voice calm. With only the two of them in the room, she could bluff. "Predicted? Forgive my ignorance, m'lord." After all, the person behind the bandages should have no understanding of caltrops or of Hawkwood.

"Katherine," Thomas chided. "Caltrops. Small, sharp spikes. Hundreds of years ago, Roman soldiers used to scatter them on the ground to break up cavalry charges. Certainly you should know. After all, you left the letter with those instructions for me: *Go the night before and seed the earth with spikes hidden in the grass. Bulls are not shod with iron. The spikes will pierce their feet and drive them into the water.*"

"M'lord?"

Behind her bandages, beads of sweat began to form on Katherine's face.

"Katherine..." He used patient exasperation, a parent humoring a dull child. "We are friends, remember? You need not keep up the pretense. After all, your letter told me how to bring dogs to a frenzy. How to force bats to their deaths in daylight. I doubt it was coincidence that help was offered to me after I told you directly that I needed it and wanted it."

Hawkwood had been right about the risk.

"M'lord?"

Thomas stood. The small dog rose too and wagged its tail.

Thomas reached down and scratched the dog's head. "Yesterday, this dog was, to all appearances, dead."

"I'm trying to understand this conversation," Katherine said.

"And I am trying to make sense of this fortress of stone. I walk through it daily, and the walls are solid. Yet it feels too often as though I walk through shrouds of mist, where nothing is as it appears. Including you."

"M'lord?" She felt panicked and trapped and could think of no other response.

"There's a potion of medicinal herbs and roots. One known to very, very few. Administered in too strong a dose, it kills like a poison. But in the right dosage, it renders a person so close to death that it is almost impossible to tell the difference."

He stepped closer, examining her mask closely. She stepped back.

He spoke quietly. "Twice, if I am not mistaken, I have been fooled by the apparent death of a woman. The first was the daughter of the former lord of Magnus. And the second was the death of an old woman, the herbalist who visited Magnus on occasion."

He smiled, but with a coldness that chilled her. "Yet I wonder if perhaps it was the same woman?"

"I have no answer, m'lord. I am baffled at your musings."

"I don't think so." He stepped closer, and she edged away again. "You were once about to tell me what you knew about Druids, but

Geoffrey prevented it. And while you were unconscious, the potion was administered and you were taken away, dead. Then you spied on me and Magnus as the old woman herbalist."

"No!" Katherine's denial was emphatic.

"I've already sent out guards to find the old man who posed as your husband," Thomas said. "But he has disappeared. So that leaves you. Isabelle."

Thomas lifted a hand to her bandaged face.

"No!" she cried. "You cannot shed light upon my face! It is too hideous."

Thomas dropped his hand. "These are your choices. Unwrap it yourself. Let me unwrap it. Or, if you struggle, the guards will be called to hold you down. They will also be witnesses…something I'll wager you do not wish."

Katherine whimpered, something she had learned to do well over the years. "Thomas…the humiliation. How can you force me to—"

"I shall count to three. Then I call the guards."

He stared at her, cold and serious.

Katherine firmed her chin. "I shall do it myself."

It seemed a dream, to be within Magnus and finally removing the hated mask. Wrap by wrap, she removed the cloth around her face. When she finished, she shook her hair free. And waited, defiant.

"It… It…" He found his voice. "It is *you*."

FORTY-NINE

Y ou did that in the moonlight, once," Thomas said with wonder in his voice. "You loosed your hair and gazed at me directly thus. I shall never forget."

Confusion. *Do I feel anger or relief?* Katherine showed neither. Merely waited.

"Please," Thomas said gently. "Sit and talk. I need to make sense of this. I was convinced you were Isabelle beneath the mask."

"You had seen the two of us together before you conquered Magnus."

"It would have been easy for her to hire someone to briefly wear the mask when she was not wearing it. At least that's what I told myself."

She remained standing. "How long did you know I was not who I pretended to be?"

He shook his head. "How long did I suspect? Since you arrived back as Katherine beneath those bandages. That is your name? Katherine?"

She nodded. He smiled.

He is not raging at the deception?

"Were you the herbalist in my camp?"

"Yes," she said. "But only with your best interests in mind. I was there to protect you."

"And the old man who spoke to me at night. The other herbalist?"

She nodded. He thought about it, then spoke again.

"Your disappearance the night after I conquered Magnus," Thomas began. "At first, I thought the soldiers had killed you and hidden the body. There could be no other explanation. After all, I had promised you anything if Magnus was won."

I remember that well, Katherine thought. *I remember wishing for something you could never give to a freak behind bandages—the love between a man and woman.*

"When you returned, unharmed, so much later, I could not think of a reason why you would remain away from Magnus so long, knowing I had conquered it. But I did not want to ask."

"Yes," Katherine said, "you cut me short when I tried to explain."

"I had been lied to already," Thomas said, "by someone whose beauty nearly matches yours."

"Isabelle. You thought of her often while waiting in the dungeon."

"I did," Thomas said. "She was a lesson well learned. Mere admiration of beauty does not make love. Mere beauty does not make a person whole. I confess, however, to have learned feelings for you as the Katherine behind the mask—" He stopped himself and his voice hardened slightly. "Yet you are as deceptive as she."

"Thomas—"

He did not let her finish. "And there was your unexplained entrance into Magnus. Since the night you disappeared, all guards at the drawbridge had instructions to watch for one whose face was hidden by bandages. I hoped always for your return. Yet, when you finally arrived, no guard noticed. Thus, I was forced to conclude you had entered as you are now. Unmasked."

Katherine did not protest. Better that he did not know the truth.

"So," Thomas said, "I pretended trust. I wanted to learn more about you, and playing the fool seemed the best way. I thought honey would work better than vinegar."

He held up a hand to forestall her reply. "Finally," Thomas said, "you were able to appear within Magnus, even during a siege.

Since it would be impossible for you to leave or enter with an army camped around us, I decided you had been here before the siege began. As, of course, Katherine."

Once again, she managed not to betray her thoughts. *He cannot know the truth about my escape, or my visit, then, to Hawkwood during the siege.*

So she said, "You are not filled with anger at my deception?"

Thomas smiled. "Not yet."

Katherine felt a skip in her chest. *Not yet.*

Sadness and joy tinged his smile as he spoke again.

"Katherine," he said, "I learned to know you before you spellbound me beneath a midnight moon. And you brought me instructions that saved Magnus. It is much easier to believe you are not an enemy."

"I am not," she said quickly. "How can I convince you of that?"

"Tell me about the old man. Tell me about the mission he has placed upon my shoulders. Tell me why you endured endless years in the horror of disguise."

She said nothing.

"In my bedchamber," he said, "I have found threads at the rough edge of the fireplace, threads of the material of clothing from an intruder who entered and escaped at will. I know that, somehow, there is a secret way in and out of this chamber. But I cannot find it. Is this fortress of mist riddled with chambers?"

She maintained her level gaze and hoped nothing on her face gave him any sense of whether she knew of the passages.

His voice grew urgent, almost passionate. "Tell me the secret of Magnus!"

Many more long moments of silence. Many long moments of wanting to trust, wanting to tell him everything.

But she could not. There was Hawkwood and his instructions. *"The stakes are far too great.... Love cannot cloud your judgment of the situation."*

Finally, and very slowly, she shook her head. "I cannot."

Thomas sighed. "As I thought. But even now, I cannot find anger."

She moved toward him and placed a hand on his arm. "Please..."

"No," he said with sadness. "I know so little. All I can cling to is the memory of someone who gave me the key to Magnus, and the reason to conquer. More important to Sarah than winning Magnus was a treasure of...of..."

Books, Katherine thought. *Knowledge in an age of darkness.*

"I now regret even hinting at my secret," Thomas said, "when I told you what I did the night I conquered Magnus. You will not learn about this treasure. For how I am to know you are not one of the Druids? Perhaps, by appearing to help save me from the earl, you deceive me into revealing what the Druids want most."

"Thomas, no!"

There was still sadness in his voice as he spoke. "How is it, then, that you know what the Druids do? You know the same potion to make it look as though someone is dead, just as Isabelle knows. Even astronomy, as the old man proved with his trickery at the gallows. If you are not Druids, who are you?"

That was the question she wanted to answer more than she wanted anything else in her life. But she could not.

Tears streamed shiny paths down her cheeks as she shook her head again.

"I am sorry, m'lady," Thomas said. He lifted her hand from his arm, then took some of her hair and wiped her face free of tears. "I cannot trust you. This battle—whatever it might be—I fight alone."

His touch, she thought achingly. *His eyes, now distant.*

He lifted her chin with a finger. "Remember this. I shall not forget the Katherine—the real Katherine—who comforted me in the depths of a dungeon and told me of God. Because of her, I cannot and shall not hold you, the deceiving Katherine, here against your will."

He turned away from her as he spoke his final words. "Please depart Magnus."

More great Young Adult fiction
from Sigmund

Before Magnus, Thomas was an orphan with a destiny. Catch the beginning of his journey in *The Orphan King*, book 1 of Merlin's Immortals.

When Caitlyn and her companions find themselves the prey of a terrifying enemy, they must escape from Appalachia—the nation carved from the heart of the United States after years of war—in a frantic search to understand the dark secrets behind Caitlyn's existence and her father's cruel betrayal.

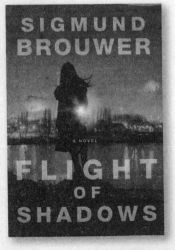

A genetically gifted teen must navigate the dangerous waters of the caste-system of a future America in search for the truth about her purpose. Meanwhile, a bloodthirsty killer is bent on revenge against her.

Read an excerpt from these books and more at www.WaterBrookMultnomah.com!